Last Hope

Mark Parada

Contents

Prologue

♥

1813: Grosvenor Square.

It's time to cast our wagers on the approaching social season, dear reader. Think about the Baron Featherington's household. Three misses were forced onto the marriage market by their taciturn, tasteless mother like wretched sows.

The widowed Viscountess Bridgerton's household may offer far greater chances. A startlingly large family renowned for their abundance of flawlessly attractive males and flawlessly gorgeous daughters.

Or maybe Abigail Bentley, who is incredibly beautiful, will emerge from the ashes to be introduced today. Can she change how her family is perceived? Or will the Bentley family's loss of the lady of the house be too great?

I appreciate you, Olivia. As her lady's maid finished adjusting her corset, Abigail replied. Once we have the slip, we can finally order the gown.

The yelling cut off Abigail. in actuality, her brothers' yelling.

"You took it!"

"No, I didn't!"

"Oh, dear God, not today." As she reached for her robe, which was sea-foam in colour, Abigail sighed.

As she left her room, she had just fastened it around her waist.

"Boys!" She spoke in a pretty severe tone that she was accustomed to by this point. Did I mention that this was the only day I needed order? I am aware that there is much hubbub right now, but if you behave well today and act like my little princes, we can do whatever you want to do tomorrow. I might even assist you in flying the new kite. Everything, even peanuts and candy floss, is available. But today, I need you to exercise restraint. Can you accomplish this for me?

She knelt down now so she could address the two directly.

"Yes, Abby." They all spoke at once.

"I appreciate you very much. Give me the horse now. She quietly extended her hand.

Benjamin gave it to you. She stood up and turned back towards her room while holding the wooden horse in her hand. Her robe was swishing at her feet.

"Abby?" Asked, she overheard Calvin.

"Yes?" Her hand was on the doorknob when she whirled around.

"So, just what are you doing today? I know it's crucial, but what exactly is it?

"I'm carrying on with my past practises. what I should carry out. I am looking after our family. Abigail then went to her room to complete getting dressed.

This day is very significant. A terrible one for some. For today is the day that Her Majesty the Queen is presented with London's misses who are interested in marriage. May God grant them eternal salvation.

From her carriage, Abigail got out. Her white gown, embellished with jewels, shone stunningly in the summertime sun. Behind her, her father took a step out. His feet briefly tripped over the step, but he was able to stop himself before falling to the ground.

Say you didn't bring the flask, please. Because Abigail was scarcely moving her lips, her whisper in her father's ear was barely audible. Always, someone was looking on.

Just in case of an emergency. Many memories of your mother surface on this day. He responded with a mutter.

"Mother's memory is evoked by everything." She was on the verge of yelling now.

The Baron looked around as he cleared his throat. Where is your aunt Edith now? He was obviously trying to change the topic.

A female family member had to be present in order to represent a young lady in court. Abigail was left alone with her father's elder sister after her mother passed away. She was very severe, but she was capable of getting the task done. If she weren't as terrifying as inferno, Abigail would have even liked her imposing presence.

Unfortunately, Abigail's aunt could only visit for the day, so she would only be present to introduce Abigail to the court and not be able to join her at any of the balls. This implied that Abby would be responsible for finding a match by herself.

However, her father was correct; her aunt was meant to meet them at the door. The debutante peered around and noticed an elderly woman leaving a carriage on her left, doing it with grace and authority. The older woman started to move towards the two Bentleys when her cain hit the ground.

"So, why are you two still standing there? I'm here, so let's go inside. She extended an arm to join Abigail and grabbed hold firmly, more for control than for support. With her father supporting the other arm, Abby inhaled deeply and moved forward.

After saying goodbye to her father, she was entering the ladies waiting room with her aunt. which was crammed to the gills with mothers and their incredibly tense-looking daughters.

Is there nowhere to sit, my god? Her aunt murmured as she entered the space a little bit more. Sighing, Abigail followed the woman as she made her way to seats that were already, very obviously, taken. "You. Up." As she said this, Daphne Bridgerton, who was nearby, was targeted by the woman's cain.

"Oh, I'm so sorry, madam." After making a courteous comment, Daphne offered the older of the two seats.

Abby quickly caught up to the conversation, "No, I'm sorry," she responded. She's a powerhouse, but that was impolite. Hello, Daphne. I've missed you.

"Abigail! I'm delighted to see you once more. She embraced her old friend and hugged him. The question "How are you?" She drew back and gave her companion a somewhat worried look. Are you feeling better now? The two hadn't seen one other since her mother's burial, when Abby was a wreck and simultaneously trying to raise her brothers for the first time.

"Thank you for asking, Daphne; I'm doing just fine." In a way, Abigail's response was automatic.

Daphne arched an eyebrow, as if sensing that her buddy had said the phrase a number of times previously but hadn't meant it. Abby chuckled.

Really, I've improved a lot. Though it's still challenging, I have everything under control. She gave her comfort.

They're almost ready for us, dear. Oh, hi Abigail. Next to her daughter, Violet Bridgerton entered the conversation.

It is "Lady Bridgerton." Abigail acknowledged him with a bow.

Please tell me it's Violet, my sweetheart. The mother took her hand in her outstretched hand. "Your mother and I were extremely close friends, my dear. You can contact me at any time if you need anything. Why don't you come for supper this week, in fact?

Oh well, I'd really like to. said Abigail. She could arrange for the nannies to watch her brothers in the evening, but it would require some work.

"Wonderful Tomorrow, I'll mail you a letter. If you'll pardon us, please. She turned her head back to her daughter. "That's us, darling."

I'll see you later, Abby. As she began to pivot, Daphne said.

Good fortune. As she left, Abigail muttered.

"Abigail!" On her left, she heard her aunt calling, so she got up to move next to her. "Are you aware of what must be done?" Uncle Edith enquired.

"At this moment or..?" Abby inquired.

obtaining your match. Do you comprehend the requirements? God help your father, he won't try to match you up with anyone. You must do it on your own and find someone to look after you and your brothers. The elderly woman spoke bluntly, without any sugar coating.

Abigail said, "Believe me. "I am fully aware of the situation and what needs to be done,"

"Good. You alone, my dear, carry the Bentley name. Love must be put aside. You are ultimately responsible for regaining your family's honour and reputation.

Abigail turned her head and gave a sombre nod.

"Yes." She grumbled. "There's no rush."

Today, just The Queen's eye is important. A young lady's value might fall to unimaginable lows with just the slightest hint of discontent. However, as we all know, a lady may burn more quickly the brightly she shines.

It is strange to walk in front of The Queen. She was nothing compared to the stern look The Queen gave her as she came down the aisle towards Her Majesty if she thought her aunt was a force to be reckoned with. Her father and two brothers were visible out of the corner of her eye, but she dared not avert her eyes. She could see that the Queen was trying her, but she wouldn't falter. Too much depended on this; too many of the things she held dear depended on her receiving Her Majesty's approval.

So, as she drew nearer to the person who had the power to make or break her future, she kept her head high and took deep, calming breaths. She had a straight back and compassionate yet hard eyes. She would seem capable.

She didn't look away until she was standing before the throne, at which point she bowed her head and body in a low curtsy. She kept it there until The Queen was ready to take action. Up till she decided whether to approve or not. She kept inhaling deeply and fixed her gaze on the ground until she heard it.

"Stand." King or Queen talked.

She therefore stood while maintaining her powerful aura.

You'll perform admirably. She nodded in agreement and predicted. She then gracefully waved her hand to indicate to Abigail that she was finished after saying those words.

"Did that really just happen?" As they turned to leave, she murmured to her aunt.

"Voice down, my dear. Keep your head up. You now have high expectations.

Chapter 1

♥

Abigail was taken aback when she opened her invitation to the Danbury ball because it was a very tough invitation to receive. Lady Danbury could be gentler than she appeared to be, Abby had a sneaky feeling.

So there she was in one of her most expensive gowns, sitting in front of her vanity as Olivia finished off her hair. Even though she was appreciative of the invitation, she was anxious about it. Not for the reasons that most debutantes would be, but rather for a factor that could seriously damage their reputation.

Her father was by far her biggest worry. Even though she was willing to shoulder the responsibility of selecting a date on her own, she was unable to go to a ball unaccompanied, so her father had to maintain enough sobriety to avoid bringing shame on herself and her family's name.

"Thank you, Olivia." Abby heaved a sigh. I'll be prepared if you could just give me my gloves.

Miss, you really do look great. As she gave her the satin gloves, Olivia informed her. Like your mother, I suppose.

Although Abigail could feel tears stinging the back of her eyes, she took a deep breath to fend them off.

"I'm grateful, Olivia. However, I must admit that if I do, it's entirely because of you. Your work on my hair was outstanding. In order to see the back of the intricate updo Olivia had curled her curls into, Abby compliment-ed and turned, keeping her back to the full-length mir-ror.

She was really lovely, and the jewelled berets she had braided into her hair made them sparkle as she caught the light. Additionally, her shape was enhanced by the dazzling pale green outfit. She did resemble her mother, as her maid had correctly noted.

As Abby put on her elbow-length gloves and left her room, she gave Olivia one more nod and grin. She peered into the night nursery to see how her brothers were doing before heading down the stairs. Both young-sters were reading picture books while their nanny sat in a chair doing needlework.

You two ought to be asleep, right? As she entered the room, she asked jokingly.

"Abby!" After yelling and setting down his book, Calvin stood up and knelt down.

"Woah! You appear to be a princess. As he observed her garment sparkle in their room's lamplight, Benjamin was in amazement.

"Why, thank you, kind sir." Abby answered with a fictitious curtsy.

"I wish we could go tonight with you!" Calvin grumbled.

After chuckling, Abby approached her younger brother.

"Someday." She kissed his forehead as she slipped the blanket around him. You two need to sleep, nevertheless, for the time being.

She moved over to Benjamin and did the same thing again.

You two have a good night. Good night, baby. With her hand on the doorknob, she muttered.

"Goodnight, miss." Abby heard as she carefully shut the door.

The debutante went down the stairs and entered the parlour to find her father. She discovered him there, downing yet another brandy.

I know today makes you think of mother, but I need you to control yourself tonight, she said, breaking the stillness in the room with a frustrated sigh.

When her father turned, it appeared as though his neck was constricting. "You, you resemble her exactly." He poured another glass while keeping his eyes closed.

He was prevented from getting another pour when Abigail quickly crossed the room and put her hand on the bottle cap.

"Listen. I am aware that you miss your mother. I concur. However, I have a task to complete, and while I am aware that I will have to work alone to complete it, you aren't making things any simpler. Just go through tonight without bringing shame to our name.

You're so competent. exactly like her. He murmured as he took her arm and reached for his coat jacket before leading the way to the ball.

They have been raised and prepared since infancy to be titled, chaste, and innocent. We'll find out tonight which young women might be able to find a partner and avoid the horrible, depressing state known as "the spinster."

Almost quickly after entering the celebration, Abigail and her father left. Abby didn't mind because it would only make her work simpler if he went somewhere else to divert his attention. Lady Bridgerton and Daphne were immediately visible to her as she turned around. She made the decision that starting with friends would be the best line of action.

"Mom, he's being impossible," he said. As Daphne joined the conversation, she overheard.

The question "Who is being impossible?" To signal her presence, Abby asked a question.

"Oh, Abigail!" Upon observing her, Violet Bridgerton gave her a short hug.

"Look, my fellow diamond, there she is." Abby was drawn in by Daphne as she gave her a brief kiss on the cheek.

"Hm?" Abby questioned while returning the smile.

"Darling, have you heard?" Violet explained in a round-about way. "They're calling you and Daphne the jewels of the season. Only you two were chosen out by the Queen. Everyone has noticed your presence, so look around.

When Abby looked around the ballroom, she noticed that practically all of the guys were giving the two debutantes stares that they undoubtedly believed to be un-obtrusive.

"Do they really believe they're doing it covertly?" Daphne chuckled as Abby refocused her gaze on her after tearing her gaze away from the crowd.

"Whose opinion are guys to have? My brother is un-doubtedly an example of deeds that are beyond com-prehension.

"Oh?"

"Dearest." Violet said with a mild tone of caution.

"Oh, mama, kindly. It's just Abby. In response to her mother, Daphne said before turning to face her companion again.

"My dearest brother has made the decision to be really difficult this evening. He won't let me dance with anyone, not even him. Daphne exploded.

"Well, he must be a man, that's why. No person not of the female sex could comprehend what we must do. Violet and Daphne laughed at what Abigail said. Despite the fact that he must have left you alone for so long, where is he?

"Actually on the way." Daphne murmured as she cast a glance in the general direction of the person Abby assumed to be her brother.

She followed her gaze and saw a man coming straight at them. Abby gasped for air. Of course, she had already known Anthony. Before her mother died, and before taking care of her home and raising her brothers occupied all of her time. Physically, he appeared to be about the same, but there was something about the way he carried himself today, or perhaps it was simply that courtship and marriage were on her mind that made him look so very alluring.

She had no idea that as he approached the trio of three, similar things were going through his mind. Of fact, he already recognised her, but all of a sudden, she appeared older, more like a woman than a teenager. She carried herself differently, but he was unable to describe why. Naturally, he would never express these sentiments or even acknowledge them to himself. Because he recalled Sienna and how he had promised to ignore everyone when he had broken up with her. No, he came to support his sister.

"Mother, sister." He said to say hello.

Daphne remarked, not bothering to mask her irritation, "Anthony." You may recall Abigail Bentley.

"Yes, hello, how are you?" He formally enquired.

I'm doing great, thank you. She replied in a similarly formal manner.

That game allowed two players. And if there was anything Abigail knew how to do, it was conceal her genuine emotions.

Please pardon me, Miss Bridgerton, but I'd want to take a dance from you. A tall, good-looking man approached the four and offered Daphne his hand.

The answer is "Yes, you may." As her brother started to argue, Daphne spoke up pretty forcefully. He promptly took her by the hand and led her away.

"Now," Violet commenced. She may have been trying to settle her kid down before he had a chance to become irate, Abby had a sneaky hunch. You two nice young people can't just stand around like a pair of mallards, can we? You two are off!" She made a definite motion towards the dance floor.

Well, I'm not, I guess. Abigail interrupted Anthony as he began by saying, "Oh, I don't think--"

They both stopped talking and looked at each other after realising they had spoken over each other. Although that made them feel bad, Lady Bridgerton, who was standing next to them, thought it was adorable.

"You two are nonsense. You're off now. She gently prodded each one.

Anthony obediently took Abigail's hand and led her onto the dance floor as she was about to resist once more. They entered the waltz style that the other visitors were participating in. They took an even step with both feet in sync with the music. Naturally, they had all been raised for it, so they were accustomed to it at this point.

I'm sorry, but my mother had me come to you. He started talking.

If he were being completely honest, which of course he wasn't, he would say that he had actually relished having a reason to dance, especially with her.

It's fine, actually. She responded, quick on her feet as the attractive Bridgerton guided her around the dance floor. "However, I suspect you'd prefer not to be here at all."

She silently cursed herself because she probably shouldn't have said it because her words often escape her control. She would have to exercise restraint there.

"Oh my lord, I should not have—" She began, but Anthony interrupted her.

"No, thanks. Actually, you're right. He spoke.

He took note of her directness and you could just make out the faintest hint of a smirk on his face.

"If it weren't for my sister, I wouldn't be here."

Whether we desire to be here or not, balls like these frequently show to be necessary. Consider your own life, she urged.

When the music stopped and everyone else stood up to bow and curtsy to one another, Anthony was going to ask what she was referring to. Abigail was the first to speak as the couple imitated people around them.

"Well, it was beautiful," But the sound of glass smashing and a chair loudly scraping interrupted her.

Abigail noticed her father as they both turned to face the ruckus.

She quickly moved in the direction of her father, who it turned out was the one who had started the disturbance, while she mumbled the French curse, "Merde."

He had a broken champagne glass in his hand and was slightly slouched in a chair. When she finally got to him, she grabbed his hand firmly and pulled him up.

"Father. You appear ill; let's take you home. In an attempt to dispel the rumours, she spoke in a fairly strained manner yet loudly enough for everyone to hear.

She could pretend he was ill as long as no one came too close, but because she was standing right next to him, she could smell the alcohol on him. She decided to leave the celebration early and lead her father out of the ballroom, heaving a long, heavy sigh as she did so while fiercely grinning at anyone who noticed.

She failed to see, though, that Anthony Bridgerton had followed her out. He couldn't place it, but there was something about her. an aura of self-assurance and wisdom. It was intriguing, but he wasn't sure.

However, he was quickly distracted from his thoughts when he recognised the distinct sounds of an old buddy of his. He turned after taking one more glance at the Bentleys departing the ballroom to discover his old friend Hastings speaking to his sister. In order to stop them, he moved quickly, temporarily forgetting his perplexing feelings towards the woman he had danced with.

Chapter 2

♥

In an unladylike manner, Abigail snorted at the final few phrases. The last thing Lady Featherington would want is for anyone to be receiving all the attention save her daughters.

She was walking after her brothers in the park as they ran erratically in front of her with their new kite while holding the most recent issue of Whistledown in her hand. She watched them try to get some breeze and wondered what was in it.

She had been gone all day with her brothers and hadn't noticed that her drawing room was empty. Instead, she had told the maids to collect any deliveries and messages and asked them to call on her later.

Her brothers reminded her of her promise of a kite-flying, peanut-eating, and candy-floss-getting day, but she was unable to be there in person to welcome them. Of course, a promise was a promise, and in all honesty, she preferred being with them outside than being in her stuffy drawing room with suitors who only wanted to use her as a walking incubator.

She ought to be more eager and interested in potential suitors. She had to do that—it was her job. She had to do it to provide for her family. She wished she could be more like Daphne who really wanted these things. A family of her own, someone to love, etc., but at this particular time, Abigail's only perception of marriage was that it was a need. She had to do it; it wasn't something she wanted to do.

She had sympathy for Daphne, to be specific. Knowing how badly she desired this, she must have been upset by the vacant drawing room and even more so by the news of it. She worried about the time as she suddenly recalled she was supposed to join them for supper tonight.

Please pardon me, sir, but I need to bother you right now. She halted a bystander. It was half past three, he informed her after taking off his pocket watch.

She thanked him and started to trot to catch up to her brothers, silently cursing in French. The kite was now actually flying.

, "Abby, look!" While Benjamin was in control, Calvin said.

"You two are amazing! Well done!" She commended. But I have to go home and get ready for dinner with the Bridgertons, so I'm afraid we have to take it down immediately.

"But you promised, and we haven't even had candy floss yet!" Calvin continued while Benjamin sipped.

"Yes, Abby, we were excellent yesterday."

She knelt down to look Calvin in the eye as Ben lowered the kite, saying, "You were both very charming yesterday, I'm so proud of you." Standing, she turned to face Benjamin. And you're right, I did promise candy floss; I did deliver. Therefore, we must hurry and buy some on the way home. They both extended their hands in response to her request. They joined in rhythm as she started to skip, which caused them to laugh.

"Ah, the Bridgertons are there now actually." As soon as she noticed Daphne and Anthony riding extremely close by, she said stopping.

Wow, horses. Calvin remarked and slipped free of her hold before sprinting off in the general direction of the Bridgertons.

"Calvin!" Ben was still in her other hand as she said and started running after him.

"Woah!" As Calvin drew near to them and his horse came to a stop, she overheard Anthony exclaim.

"Calvin, hello! Never again flee in such manner. She grabbed both of his shoulders and spoke forcefully before looking him in the eye.

Sorry Abby, but those horses are beautiful. He gestured at the riding siblings pretty angrily.

She turned to face Daphne and Anthony while standing at her tallest point.

He has a fascination for horses, so I'm really sad. Can he pet one of them? She questioned in an apology-laden manner.

"But obviously!" said Anthony. "Go ahead and pet my Guardian," I said.

With wide eyes, Calvin approached the animal and started to stroke his neck. He grinned even larger and placed both of his small hands on the horse to further express his affection for it.

Not fair, I say. I also want to pet the horses. Abby rolled her eyes at what Benjamin stated.

That's no problem; feel free to visit and pet Pearl, my pet. On her own, cream-colored horse, Daphne said while riding behind her brother.

Ben grinned and rushed over the horses' backs to pet Daphne.

"Thank you, you just made their day." Sincere words from Abigail.

When her brother spoke before Daphne, she lost her opportunity to respond.

It's truly not a problem. He spoke while sporting a broad grin and casting a glance between Abby and her brother.

Daphne looked at her brother, who was being unusually accommodating. She had never witnessed him happier to chat to someone except his family before, despite the fact that he obviously liked kids. She turned to look at him and Abby while suddenly flashing a sly grin.

Right, well, if we're going to see you for dinner this evening, we'd better get going, and you should too. said Daphne.

Antony raised an eyebrow at this and turned to face his sister.

Abigail answered, "Right of course," taking Calvin's hand without pausing to take notice of anything. "Ben, follow me. Hello tomorrow night.

She turned around and left with her two siblings to get their treats and go home.

Daphne and her brother kept their horses running.

Anthony reacted swiftly and remarked to his sister, "You didn't tell me she was coming for dinner."

Did I not? Smirking, Daphne enquired before clicking her tongue to move her horse more quickly.

Anthony glared angrily at his sister. In all honesty, he wasn't sure why he was upset that he wasn't made aware of this. He ought to be, if anything, disinterested. Nevertheless, there he was, agitated over her visit. He refused to think about or question these emotions, so he shook them off. Without a doubt, given enough time, they would slow down and leave. However, that was not to be. He had no idea that his feelings for the stunning Bentley woman would only intensify with time.

Chapter 3

♥

Anthony rushed out of the dining room when he saw whose place card he was seated next to, and more particularly whose place card was seated next to Daphne's.

"Mother!" He called, entering the foyer.

"In here, dearest!" He heard from the parlor.

He headed that way, hot footed.

"Did you not think to tell me we had guests for dinner? More particularly did you not think to tell me that the guests were Hastings and Miss Bentley?" He questioned his mother, who was quite apparently caught off guard.

"W-well the Duke is coming because Lady Danbury told me of his fondness for gooseberry pie, and Mrs. Porter is renowned for that dish." Violet explained to her eldest son, clearly not expecting this level of irritation.

"No, you are attempting to set Daphne up with Simon and I am telling you now, it won't work. He has absolute-ly no intention of marrying, he's told me himself." He rebutted. "And you still have yet to explain why Abigail has received an invitation for tonight."

"Oh please if I had a shilling for every time a man swore he would never get married, I'd be a very rich woman." She scoffed. "And why should it matter if Abigail comes over for dinner?"

"Yes, brother. Why should it matter if Abigail comes for dinner?" Benedict began to tease from his spot on the couch.

"Ben, stop it." Anthony gritted out.

"Stop what? Have I missed something?" Hyacinth questioned as she bounced up from the table she and Gregory sat at.

"Please, you've only missed the fact that our brother has a large crush on Abby and refuses to acknowledge it." Eloise said, not even looking up from her reading.

Everyone in the room snorted simultaneously. Well, all except for Anthony.

He glared at Eloise and said, "Well, I can tell I have no grounds to refute the invitations and since I'm being teased for something untrue, I shall go up to change." With this he walked out of the room and everyone burst into laughter.

"Does he truly not see it?" Eloise questioned towards Benedict.

"In total fairness, I don't think either of them do." He responded and left the room to go change as well.

"For all we know, Whistledown may be some interloper living in Bloomsbury of all places." Colin said in response to the debate that sprung up about Lady Whistledown's identity.

"What should be so terrible about Bloomsbury? That people there actually work for a living?" Benedict countered.

"She does seem to be someone with access." Daphne added.

Abigail smiled, as dinner was in full swing and a rather lively debate had taken place. She enjoyed the warmth she felt at the company around the table. All of them at one table, even the children. It was refreshing to see such a large and happy family. She missed this, this is the feeling she remembered when her mother used to entertain her own family at dinner. It was nice to feel again.

"Who knows if Whistledown is even a she?" Colin questioned.

Abby rolled her eyes.

"Fair point." She heard Anthony say from next to her.

"Because she's simply too good to be anyone but a man?" Eloise commented back, sarcastically.

"Amen." Abigail said and further backed up Eliose's point. "The fact is that no man would write under a woman's pseudonym. He'd have too much to lose and nothing to gain. No, you're looking for a woman."

Eloise smiled, having finally been supported in an opinion at the table.

"Well I think it rather obvious the writer is Lady Danbury." Francessca said from across the table.

"Lady Danbury enjoys sharing her insults with society directly. She would never bother herself writing them all down."

"Could it be Lady Featherington?" Hyacinth posed.

"No!" Everyone says in unison.

"You have yet to read what Lady Whistledown writes of the Featheringtons, little sister."

"You know, I didn't think you'd get involved in the debate." Abby heard a lower volume speak next to her.

Turning her head towards Anthony she replied, "I agree with your sister. Taking all the facts into account, Whistledown has to be a woman."

"You shouldn't encourage her." He said a bit louder this time so that he caught Eloise's attention too. "She has an easy enough time speaking her opinion already." He was pointedly teasing his sister now, who made a face at him.

Abby turned towards Eloise and said, "It's a privilege to be able to share one's opinion, I admire you for that. Just don't waste it."

Eloise smiled and nodded, clearly with some approval.

"You speak as if you can't." Eloise pried.

"Well, haven't you heard? No man wants a woman that's forthcoming." Abby said with a mix of resentment and sarcasm dripping from her tone as she cut into her food.

"Are you truly in need of a husband that much?" Anthony wondered, then realized too late that he said it out loud. "I truly apologize, that was--"

"No." Abigail cut him off. "Believe me, I appreciate the bluntness of speech. And to answer your question, unfortunately, yes. If my mother were still alive, I wouldn't be but I have to do what's best for my family and more importantly, my brothers."

"Now that, I completely understand." He paused for a moment then said, "It's hard. Having to step into a parent's shoes. Hardest thing I've done in my life."

He reached for his wine glass.

"It's almost as if you're never sure of yourself. Like you wish to do what is right so badly and yet, you don't always know what right is." Abigail empathized.

"Exactly. I've never met anyone who's understood it before." Anthony marveled before his gaze traveled down the table and landed on the Duke and Daphne conversing.

Following his gaze, Abigail rolled her eyes and couldn't help but comment, "If I may say so, you don't seem too thrilled with your other guest this evening."

She smirked and took a bite, looking back up towards him as she had grabbed his attention yet again.

"That obvious?" He questioned.

She chuckled and nodded. "It's sort of entertaining. The protective big sibling act. I feel it too, believe me, it's just my siblings are still children. Which I suppose still brings its own set of baggage into the mix." She muttered the last part as she reached for her own wine.

"Yes, well. The Duke is my mother's doing. She's attempting to play matchmaker but I won't allow that to happen with him." Anthony stated as his eyes wandered back towards his friend and sister.

"Well from what I hear, you're not exactly making it easy for Daphne."

"Gossiping about me now are we?" He teased.

"Well, Mr. Bridgerton, you're just too fascinating not to discuss." She arched a brow as she spoke, humoring him.

They had gained some attention now from their end of the table, due to their banter, but of course they did not notice.

"Don't I have a duty to protect my sister from unwant-
ed suitors. She deserves only the best, in my eyes."

"But why is it your eyes that get to determine what is
the best? You have to remember, this is what we were
raised for. All we have been trained to do as women, and
if you continue to block your sister at every turn you will
condemn her to shame rather than protect her."

"And yet I still have a job, not just as her brother, but
as the head of this household to not only make sure she
finds a match worthy of the name but to make sure she
finds someone worthy of her."

"I will concede your intentions are honorable My Lord,
but you lack empathy. Unless you've experienced what
it is to have your only value placed upon your ability to
find a husband, then you have no room to talk."

He turned quite serious at that last comment, as
Daphne had said something similar to him in the park.

"You're the second person to point something of that
nature out to me today."

"Well then, maybe God is attempting to send you a
sign." She quipped. "Unless of course you do know what
it is I mean and I hadn't realized. Tell me, My Lord, have
you been a woman of late?"

He laughed and this ticked the mood of the conversation back up. She smiled and was about to take another

bite when she felt an elbow nudge her ribs. She turned to Eloise who was smiling with vindication at her.

"You might just be my new favorite person in the whole world."

"A high honor." Abigail chuckled and finally bit off her fork.

They both laughed.

She continued to engage in conversation until a servant came bustling into the dining room with a note for her on a platter. She took it, and unfolded it to read. By this point everyone at the table had halted conversation to see what the message was about.

"Oh god." She muttered. "If you will excuse me, Lady Bridgerton, I must leave. My youngest brother has taken ill."

"Oh darling, of course." Violet said as Abigail stood.

As she did, the men at the table stood too, as was polite.

"Let me know how he is when you can."

"Let me walk you to your carriage." Anthony said and set his napkin on the table.

Every Bridgerton sibling exchanged glances.

"Thank you very much for the dinner. Goodnight everyone." Abby made a blanket thank you.

They all chimed a goodnight back as the two swept out of the dining room.

Chapter 4

♥

Abigail read Lady Whistledown's words as she rode in her carriage to Bridgerton house. She smiled, having not attended last night's ball due to family matters, she enjoyed reading of Daphne's triumph. She deserves it, and was happy her friend found not only someone high of rank, but someone who seemed to want her for her.

Although, she must confess, Abigail was rather shocked indeed to see the line of suitors exiting the doorway of Bridgerton house. She would have expected the announcement of the Duke's intrigue to be enough for Daphne and her family. Yet, of course, she should have expected that men would be here. For men always seem to want what they cannot have. Although, this did leave her to wonder why they all seemed to be leaving at once.

Rolling her eyes slightly and laughing a bit in Olivia's direction, she reached for the side of the carriage as a footman opened the door and extended his hand for her support. She smiled as a thank you and walked forward towards the double doors. She could practically feel the gentlemen caller's eyes on her. Smirking, but keeping her head held high, she walked up the steps, not sparing them a glance. In part, because she had a task at hand and also in part, because she knew that would intrigue them more.

Chuckling to herself she nodded as Olivia headed off to the kitchen and the housekeeper began to show her up the stairs. She was on the landing when the eldest Bridgerton practically plowed past her, knocking her off balance slightly.

"Oh!" She let out as she reached for the railing but caught Mr. Bridgerton's arm instead.

"Oh, my apologies." He said as he managed to catch her, completely distracted from his anger before. "I did not expect to see you here." Realizing his hands had lingered on either arm he awkwardly pulled them back down to his sides.

She laughed rather awkwardly and said, "Um, it's quite alright. I just um, came to see your mother and sister."

Remembering the conversation, or rather the argument, he had just left with them, his face twisted back into one of annoyance and settled at a frown.

"You're quite peeved about something." She observed, arching her brow.

"Well according to many, I always am." He laughed it off.

She needn't be worried with his family drama. He knew her hands were already full with her own. It was then he noticed the small cut that grazed her left cheek.

"What happened there?" He questioned, his hand beginning to lift upwards toward it, but he stopped himself and let it drop back at his side.

It's almost as if everything seemed natural with her, and he had to stop himself from doing what felt so right under the context of polite society.

"Um. That... is quite a long story."

(The Night of the Dinner)

Her carriage door opened and she used the footman's hand to balance herself as she quickly stepped down and out, towards her front doors. As she approached the steps, the doors flung open and her housekeeper exited them, rushing towards her.

"Oh Miss thank you for coming! I'm ever so sorry to pull you away from dinner."

"It's fine Mrs. Whiler, now what exactly is the problem? The note said something about father." Abigail questioned for an explanation as the housekeeper helped her with her cloak.

She had covered quickly and told the Bridgertons it was her brother, but that was simply done with the intention to avoid scandal.

"His Lordship is um... he's not himself, Miss. I've known him for nearly twenty years now and have never seen him in such a state."

"What kind of state exactly?" Abigail had a bad feeling.

"Well he's drunk himself into quite the theatrics. We sent the boys in to say goodnight, as we always do, and he was sobbing. Harder than I've ever seen a man sob. And then, he got angry. He shouted and threw things. The boys are fine." She added upon seeing Abby's face. "But we couldn't think how to calm him, so we sent for you."

"Very well. I see I have my work cut out for me. I'm going to need some coffee in the drawing room and if I manage to convince him to go to bed, I will need help getting him there." She started to head in her intended direction when she turned around and said, "And Mrs. Whiler, not a word to anyone."

"Of course not Miss." And she too, bustled off. Leaving Abby simply standing in front of the doors to the drawing room.

Taking a deep breath, she cleared her head and twisted the doorknob.

She poked her head in first, "Father?"

"Hm." She heard him grunt out. She could just make out the top of his head on the other side of the couch as he slumped further into it.

"Father. I really think it's time we got you into bed." She had fully entered the room now and crossed its lengths to face her father, who was cradling his whiskey glass in his hand. His head lulled upward and his eyes quickly brimmed with tears.

"You look so much like her! I can't stand it!" He sobbed out.

Finding herself lacking empathy as his theatrics and emotions could cost them everything, she simply squatted, to look him in the eye and said, " We all miss mother. I know you loved her. But at the moment it's time for you to put the glass down and get to bed."

"No!" He gargled and stood suddenly.

She clenched her fists to release tension and stood as well. "Honestly, Father, I have very little patience for this. I understood the need to escape the first few months, but you have children, a life to think of! Not just Calvin and Ben but me! I am alone in the dust and you don't even care!"

She began to cry in a mixture of anger and hurt.

"How dare you-"

"How dare YOU! Do you honestly think she would have wanted you like this? Drowning in your own sorrows without as much as a glance as to the wellbeing of your family? Of her family? If she could see you now she'd be disgusted."

"Shut... UP!" He roared and threw his glass onto the ground, where it smashed its pieces violently catapulted throughout the room.

One particular glass shard reached Abigail's face and created a fresh cut across her cheek. She gasped and her hand flew up to feel the damage. It was a small cut, but when she pulled her hand back she saw the blood it drew.

"Oh, my darling, I'm so sorry."

"Go to bed Father. Now." She said with a monotonous voice.

He hung his head and left the room without another word.

Abigail took deep breaths, attempting to calm herself, but it only seemed to have the opposite effect. The more breaths she took, the quicker they came and the faster she started to hyperventilate. Collapsing onto the couch, her body became wracked with sobs. Sobs of anger, of frustration, of fear. But most of all, sobs that came with the overwhelming feeling of being truly alone.

"Needless to say I'm quite alright, just a bit uncoordinated." She smiled the memories away and made an excuse. "But I thank you for your concern. Although something tells me your 'savior complex' wishes it was more." She cringed as she realized she had said the last part out loud.

"My what now?"

"You know, I would apologize for saying that out loud, but by this point, why not when one of us says something awkward we just ignore it." She laughed.

He laughed too, not realizing how much he needed it.

"A very fair suggestion. Well, I must bid you a goodbye. You have family members of mine to see, and I have places to be. Have a lovely day, Miss Bentley." He nodded his head and with a final bright smile he left her, still on the landing.

She shook her head clear of her thoughts and began to proceed forward, up the stairs. She stood and waited as she nodded to the footman to announce her into the drawing room.

"A Miss Abigail Bentley here to see you ma'am."

"Oh Abby! Do tell her to come in" She heard Daphne say, a tone of relief in her voice.

Abigail entered the room and smiled as Violet reached to pull her into a hug.

"We were beginning to worry about you, my dear." She commented as she pulled back. "How is your brother?"

"Much better." She fibbed, smoothly. "It's good that I went though. I just came to thank you for the invitation and apologize, yet again, for leaving so abruptly."

"Oh darling, you needn't apologize. It is quite clear you have your hands full." Violet pulled her to sit on the couch. "I've been thinking and..." She paused for a moment. "What would you say to me escorting you to the balls, you could come with Daphne and Anthony and I. You could get ready here, and be a source of support for Daphne, and us to you as well."

Abigail's heart swelled, but then deflated knowing she could never accept.

"Lady Bridgerton--"

"Violet."

"Violet," She amended. "While I would love nothing more than for that to happen, you clearly have your hands full with Daphne and your other children. I couldn't ask such a thing of you."

"Well, it's a good thing you're not asking then." Daphne piped up.

"And it's a good thing we are not asking either. I will help you through this process, and bring you and Daphne out together. It's what our mother would have wanted, I'm sure of it." Violet assured her, grasping her hands to gain her full attention.

Abigail was having trouble not smiling now as her eyes filled with tears.

"Then I would love that very much." She managed out.

"Wonderful! Then it's settled! You and Daphne will be in this together."

"Mama," Daphne started. "May I have a moment with Abby?"

"Of course! I must make arrangements for your clothes and dresses to be brought here. Your Lady's maids will become fast friends. In fact, I'm sure they already are becoming so in the kitchen." The Bridgerton woman chuckled and left the room.

Once her mother had vacated the area Daphne moved over a couch to sit next to Abby and give her a much needed hug.

"Thank you for this." Abby said in her ear and then pulled away to look at her friend.

"Nonsense I wouldn't have it any other way." Daphne assured her. "As a matter of fact, I'm sort of glad to have someone I can confide in."

"Oh, the mysterious Daphne Bridgerton has secrets, let's hear them." She teased.

"In all seriousness Abby, I need help. We used to share everything, you and I, I'd like to go back to that." Said Daphne.

Abigail sat up straight, "I'd like that too."

"Alright then." Daphne stood and began pacing. This signaled to Abby that she was clearly very concerned about something. "I have a problem. My brother," She rolled her eyes at the mention of her sibling. "Has promised me to Nigel Berbrooke."

"Oh good God!" Abby exclaimed.

"Exactly. My brother is convinced he is harmless, but I know different. He snuck up on me, in the gardens at last night's ball."

"Oh Daphne... what did you do?"

"You see, here's the problem. I may have punched him."

At this Abigail couldn't stop herself before she snorted, rather unladylike, and her hand flew to her mouth as she suppressed laughter.

"It isn't funny!" Daphne said in exasperation.

"It's a little funny. I would hope that taught him something, but I imagine he's acting like it never happened." Abby wagered.

"Precisely. Well, once that cow fell unconscious in the grass... that's when the Duke came in."

"Ah I see. My, my, Daphne you had quite the salacious night didn't you?"

"You're still teasing."

"Sorry. Continue."

Daphne moved to sit next to Abigail on the couch again and looked her directly in the eye.

"The Duke and I... have an arrangement. He is pretending to court me so I can interest more suitors and he can keep ambitious mothers off of his back. Now, the only problem is Anthony and Berbrooke won't take no for an answer, and I have to rely on the Duke to look interested enough so that they will take his intentions seriously. The problem is, he isn't serious. It's all a ruse." Daphne spouted out. It seemed as if she was on the verge of expelling the contents of breakfast as she finally slumped back into the couch.

Abigail was quiet for several moments before she finally said, "My goodness, that is a lot of information to get in thirty seconds."

"Is that all you have to say?!" Daphne through her arms in the air.

"No, of course not. The major obstacle I see here is it's quite clear Lord Berbrooke will only accept a man's word. So either we have to do what you said, and wait for him to believe the Duke's intentions. Or, we could tell your brother of the attempt in the garden."

"No." Daphne said with finality. "He has continually ignored my wishes, I cannot be certain he would believe me. He'd only see it as complaining, or an attempt to get out of the proposal."

Abigail had a sneaking suspicion that wasn't true, but she could see where Daphne was coming from.

"Alright then. There is quite literally nothing we can do until something happens next, good or bad." She leaned back against the couch and mimicked Daphne's position.

"I hate the world we live in." Daphne said, disgruntled.

"You and me both."

"Abigail?"

"Hm?"

"What did happen to your cheek?"

Chapter 5

Abigail stood in Daphne's bedroom in front of one of the two mirrors. Also in the room were Lady Bridgerton, Eloise, Hyacinth, and Daphne's lady's maid Rose, as well as her maid Olivia.

"The sapphires, Miss?" She heard Olivia ask and turned to look at the diamond encrusted sapphire earrings and necklace set she held out.

"Yes, please Olivia."

"Oh sapphires will go lovely with that shade of blue Abigail." Violet commented which made Abby smile as she began to take the earrings from her maid.

Her dress was a pale, maya blue with glittering beads lacing the outer layer of her skirt and bodice. Lady Bridgerton was correct, her sapphires would work nicely.

"May I see?" She heard Hyacinth say, popping up from the bench she sat on.

"Of course." Abby held the earrings out in her palm and the ten year old leaned over to view them as they sparkled in the candlelight.

"Whoa, those are gorgeous!" She exclaimed.

Abby chuckled and said, "Why thank you. They were my mother's." She put them through the holes on each lobe, then moved to lift the bottom half of her updo so Olivia could put the necklace on.

"Will it be the pearls or the rubies for you, miss?" She heard Rose question Daphne.

"Oh the pearls, of course." Violet answered.

"Mama, perhaps the rubies might catch the attention of even more new suitors?"

Abigail let her hair down as Olivia finished clasping and glanced over to see Violet and Rose look at her friend with an odd expression.

"If I am not to put all my eggs in one basket, I must.. collect more... eggs." Daphne rambled and they all laughed.

"I agree with Daphne, the rubies look lovely, and we surely shouldn't leave everything up to the men." Abigail commented, knowing precisely why Daphne had chosen the rubies.

She and Daphne had covered quite a bit earlier that day. After Daphne had told her about the Duke, she inquired about the small cut on Abigail's cheek. After which, Abby practically tumbled out everything that was happening at home. Between her father and her brothers and how she basically felt like she was holding her family's reputation together with two hands.

Once Daphne had listened all the way through and took a moment to contemplate, she eventually said how fortunate it was that she was under the Bridgerton's protection now, and that she wouldn't let anything go wrong pertaining to the Bentley name. Abigail couldn't agree more. Every moment she spent with the family was further confirmation at how grateful she was to not have to be alone anymore.

At that moment, Abigail's focus was snapped back to reality when their housekeeper came bustling into the room, looking out of breath.

"Good heavens, what is it Mrs. Wilson?" Violet questioned.

"The Queen Ma'am." She responded, catching her breath.

"Has she fallen ill?"

"Has king George caused her harm?"

"Her majesty's royal stationery." Abigail noticed.

"She has written to you, my lady."

The room fell silent as Lady Bridgerton took the note, slowly. Then quickly, as if reality was catching up to her, she hurriedly unfolded the paper.

"What does it say mama?" Hyacinth piped up.

Reading it over, Violet stuttered out, "I-I am invited to a private tea with The Queen in two days' time." Laughing with glee, she turned to Daphne and said, "Never mind the pearls, you shall wear the family diamonds tonight."

Daphne turned back towards the mirror and caught Abigail's eye in it as she sat on the bench at the end of the bed, slipping on her shoes. Daphne smiled with glee as Abigail mock bowed, causing her friend to laugh.

The carriage Abby, Daphne, and Violet were riding in pulled up, in front of the rather large and grand house the ball was to take place at. Abigail let Daphne exit first and was urged to go second by Violet.

She stepped down, using the footman's hand to balance her and was greeted with Benedict Bridgerton in front of her, holding his arm out for her to take.

She took it as she asked, "Don't you have to escort your mother inside?" She glanced back towards Lady Bridgerton.

"Nah, Colin can handle that. Besides, if I were to escort her, I'd only be listening to the most updated list of eligible young ladies to dance with tonight. Something tells me a conversation with you would be much less excruciating." He laughed quietly

"Well, I shall try to live up to that expectation. I can't thank your family enough for allowing me to come out with Daphne."

"Please, of all the people we could be helping I'm ever so glad it's you. I know what it's like to lose a parent right when you need them."

She smiled up at him, thankful to speak with someone who understood.

"Abigail darling," She heard Violet say behind her and turned her head as she continued to walk. "Once we get inside, I'll introduce you to some friends of mine. Judging on how lovely you look tonight, it certainly shouldn't take long before your dance card should be full."

Abigail smiled and was blushing when she heard what sounded like a disgruntled groan come from Anthony, ahead of her. But she must have imagined it, for a minute later he was simply clearing his throat.

They all entered the party at once, and Abby's face twisted into a smile as she took at the glittering lights and bustling dancers of the ballroom. She could practically feel the eyes of everyone on them as they arrived. She guessed this is what it must feel like to be a Bridgerton. The group approached the Duke and Lady Danbury.

"A dance, Miss Bridgerton?" The Duke offered his hand.

Before Anthony could intervene Lady Danbury spoke up.

"I shall need someone else to seek me a glass of ratafia, then. Lord Bridgerton... do me the honor?"

"Of course Lady Danbury." Anthony forced a smile

Abigail smiled and began to suppress her laughter. She could feel Benedict do the same and she glanced up at him. As they made eye contact that only seemed to make it worse, and they were both now working very hard not to laugh out loud at the eldest Bridgerton's misfortunes.

It was then that Violet pulled Abigail away to introduce her to some of her friends, as well as their very handsome sons.

Abigail ended up dancing with several very handsome, and very kind young men; and not long after, had a rather full dance card.

Once she had finished the final name on the list, she pulled herself over to a table filled with drinks and took a flute of champagne, desperate for some liquid as she was now rather out of breath. She smiled as she watched the dancers on the floor and couldn't help but feel rather pleased with how she had done tonight.

She had managed several dances and lovely conversations with many young men from influential families. It finally seemed as if she might be able to get her family's reputation back on track.

It was then she heard the rather carrying whisper of Lady Featherington and Lady Cowper. "Do you suppose the Bridgertons took pity on her?"

"Well, what else could it have been? Why would an influential family such as theirs tarnish their image with that of the Bentley's?"

"Such a shame too. They used to be the most renowned family of the ton. Now her father's simply too drunk to stand, let alone raise his children."

She heard them giggling as her hand gripped her champagne flute so hard she was surprised the crystal hadn't smashed between her fingers. Before she did anything irrational, however, Lady Danbury approached her and stole her attention away.

"I knew your mother well." She started, abruptly. Lady Danbury didn't waste time with introductions. "She used to come to my game nights. Always one of the most striking people in the room."

"That's very kind of you to say Lady Danbury." Abigail responded.

"Tis not kind my girl, it's the truth. You are much more like her than you think. You are strong, just like she was. And you mustn't let the idiotic members of the ton get to you. All you can do is your best, and she would be proud." She then turned and left as abruptly as she came.

Her words filled Abigail with a sense of strength and pride. She smiled, knowing that the lady was a lot more empathetic than she let on.

Rather quickly, though, she was pulled from her thoughts as she heard ill-tempered whispering to her left. She looked through the crowd and saw a very confrontational conversation between Anthony and Lord Berbrooke as the Duke appeared to be restraining Anthony slightly, so as not to cause a scene.

Knowing precisely what this was about, her eyes scanned the dance floor and found Daphne finishing a dance with her brother. She set her champagne down and swiftly moved across the ballroom to approach her friend. She gets to them right as Daphne curtsies and her brother bows.

"Daphne, have you seen what is going on?" Her tone reaching barely above a whisper as she gestures her head towards the conversation she had just witnessed.

Daphne's eyes soon held a worried look and she quickly grabbed Abigail's hand and pulled her along as she approached Anthony.

"What has happened? Brother?"

He glanced between the two and said, "You need not worry about Berbrooke, Sister, it is done."

He sighed deeply and angrily headed away from them, and out of the ballroom. As Daphne went towards the Duke to question him, Abby couldn't help but look after where Anthony had exited. She knew she shouldn't but she simply couldn't stop herself from following him.

Leaving the room, she entered a hallway and looked to her right and left. Not seeing him, she decided on right and headed in that direction. It was there, at the end of the hall that she found him in the library. Not having noticed her arrival, he leaned over a table and seemed to be calming himself.

She stood there for a moment and watched his chest rise and fall with every deep breath he was taking. Realizing she'd been watching him for quite some time she decided to announce her presence.

"You really have quite the temper, don't you?"

Chapter 6

"**I**f you have come in here to chastise me, please don't." Anthony requested in a groan after he had turned to look at the Bentley woman standing in the doorway.

"I came in here to check on you." Abigail said, her voice remaining calm. She had some experience with angry emotions, and the best way to extinguish the fire was typically to keep a level head. "You seem rather upset, I'd simply like to make sure you don't do anything irrational."

"Well of course I'm upset," He began to pace the lengths of the library. "That horrid man made an attempt on my sister!"

"Mhm." She acknowledged and leaned against the door frame with her arms crossed.

"Wait a moment, you act as if you knew." He stopped pacing to look her in the eye.

"I did know." She responded, keeping her even keel.

"How could you not tell me?! Or convince Daphne to tell me?" He questioned, frustratedly

"I suggested that," Abigail defended. "She was convinced you wouldn't believe her."

"How could she think such a thing?" He breathed out, still seething.

"Well, I could follow her logic considering your willingness to take over her life and ignore her wishes."

"Abigail--"

"Your intentions are honorable, Anthony," She cut him off. "You wish to protect your sister, but have you ever stopped for a moment to consider that men will act very differently in front of you than they will in front of us." Abandoning logic, she began to feel growingly frustrated with his consistent oblivion.

"Tell me the truth, if Daphne had come to you, and told you what happened, would you have believed her? Or did you only accept the veracity of those claims because the Duke said them ?" She stepped further into the room.

"How dare you." He stepped forward as well, his voice in a forced calm. "You do not know me, Abigail. I protect my family, they come above all else!"

"Oh sure, you protect them but you don't listen to them. You will never know what it is like to walk through mine nor Daphne's shoes, so don't pretend for one minute you were acting in her best interests!" She spoke sternly, on the verge of shouting.

"How dare you!" They were practically face to face now. "I want the best for my sister, I care what happens to her! I care what happens to you!"

It was that last sentence that halted conversation. That, and the fact that they both became aware of how close they were to each other. They both looked with fury into each other's eyes.   Soon, however, the fury melted away and all that was left was passion. Each of their eyes flicking towards each other's lips, they both wanted to give in so badly. Their breathing was heavy and their eyes both shared a yearning for one another. Yet still, Abigail intervened before anything went too far from recovery.

"I- um" She cleared her throat and stepped a half foot back. Anthony's arm moved to catch her's, to stop her, but it stopped itself, only raised slightly above his side. "I spoke out of turn."

"As did I." Anthony responded.

He could feel the sinking feeling in his chest, although it could be for a multitude of reasons. For the feelings he felt for the woman before him, for the lack of re- membrance of Sienna, or for the regret that things had stopped when they did. He wouldn't admit it, but he suspected it was the latter.

"We- um. We shouldn't even be in here alone." She looked around the room, truly taking in her surroundings.

"No." He said, as if he just realized this.

"Dear God, okay." Her hand reached up and touched her forehead, as if this would make her think of a solution. "I'm going back into the ballroom first, you... wait here. And don't follow me in right away." With one last fleeting glance at him, she exited the room.

Leaving the eldest Bridgerton to stare at the spot she had just vacated, a million thoughts rambling through his head.

Chapter 7

Abigail finished reading the gossip sheet out loud to Olivia as she applied rouge to her cheeks.

"Wonderful," she said sarcastically. "So everyone knows. They all know my family is inches from ruin."

"The Bentley name is a respectable one within the community," Olivia assured her as she met her eye in the mirror and began applying the pink powder to her other cheek. "Your reputation is not tarnished, and you need to stop worrying. That gossiping writer only said that last bit to cause intrigue."

"But she is right," Abby conversed, standing to take her robe off to get her corset on. "I cannot have this go wrong."

Olivia began tightening the strings. "Then we shan't let it."

Once the corset was on, Abigail sent Olivia to check on her brothers as they were getting ready themselves with their nanny. They were to attend the grand picnic with the Bridgertons that day. Which, of course, made both of her brothers happy as they would be able to play with Gregory and Hyacinth.

She was glad to see they were pleased, she knew they loved the park and they really did need some friends to play with, now more than ever. Neither of them were in boarding school yet, and they were consistently surrounded by the cloud that was their mother's absence in the home.

Abigail looked up into her full length mirror. She was just in her corset and her bloomers, and there was oddly something freeing about it. Something strengthening. She stood there, in a very raw and empowering form, and looked herself in the eye.

"You can do this. You are going to do this." Her mind began to drift back to the other night in the library with Anthony.

It was exhilarating and intense, and on some level, she was sad she had stopped it when she did. But she quickly cut off her train of thought, she didn't have time for this.

Let it be known, dear reader, that if this bizarre behavior portends yet another scandal, then be sure I shall uncover it, for there is nothing like an excursion into nature to lift the spirits and loosen the tongue.

Abigail walked through the park and headed to the lakeside with her brothers bounding ahead of her. She smiled as she watched them attempt to race the birds in the sky and only pulled them back when they began to approach the many camps set up by the members of the ton.

"Ben! Cal!" She called and they turned around. She gestured her arms to reel them back and took their hands.

They were almost there when Ben asked, "May we be able to play today Abby?"

"Of course! We're in the park you should always play here, why-ever would you ask?" She looked down at him.

"Well today is important, isn't it?" He asked

"Everyday is important, Ben. You need to do what makes you happy. And if that is playing in the park, then I say go right ahead." She smiled and pushed him forward to approach the Bridgerton children who were behind their tent.

He and his brother ran forward and watched in awe as Anthony caught a hoop Gregory threw.

"Ah, I remember you two!" He said as the two Bentley brothers approached.

"Hello sir!" Calvin piped up.

"Oh there's no need to call me that, I'm Anthony." He said and tipped his hat, then handed Ben the hoop he had caught. Benjamin ran off with Gregory, and Abigail watched as Anthony bent down to whisper something in Calvin's ear.

Calvin then looked with wide eyes at the table full of sweets and ran toward it with excitement.

"Ahem." Abigail cleared her throat pointedly and the boy froze with his hand outstretched.

"Please Abby!" He whined.

"Alright, one." She said. But when he gave her a pout she amended. "Okay, two. But that's it!"

He smiled with two pastries in hand and ran off. Abigail turned to look Anthony in the eye and he gave a shrug of feigned innocence. Abby shook her head and smiled.

"Oh Abigail, good you're here!" Violet said and walked over to embrace her. Giving her a hug, she leaned back and grasped her shoulders. "Let's get you some tea, hm? I want to hear all about the gentlemen you danced with last night."

Abigail smiled and ignored the fact that Anthony shifted uncomfortably in the corner of her vision. She didn't have time to wait for him to figure his life out, no matter what feelings might have been shared last night. She moved to follow Violet as he went to sit next to his sister.

"So, your dance card certainly seemed full did it not?" Violet asked and handed her a cup of tea.

She chuckled, "Yes it seemed to be. I must confess my feet were rather sore at the end of the night."

Violet laughed and she heard a voice from her right speak. "Lady Whistledown has certainly been giving you high praise." It was Benedict.

"Ah I was wondering when I'd hear from you." She teased as she looked down to see him sitting in the chair next to her.

Behind him she saw Daphne approaching the Duke and looked to see that her seat had been vacated and just Anthony sat there, quite apparently lost in his thoughts. As though he could feel her gaze, however, he lifted his head and met her eye. They were both clearly communicating with one another, only one could not understand what the other was trying to say. It was as if there was a roadblock, an impenetrable force stopping them from truly talking with each other. About last night, about their feelings, about anything. She removed her gaze quickly as she realized she never acknowledged Benedict's comment.

"Don't even mention Whistledown." She sighed and redirected her focus back on the Bridgerton next to her. "I'm growing rather sick of what she writes."

"Don't let Eloise hear you, she's done nothing but praise her work. Speaking of, where has she gotten to?" Benedict looked around the park vaguely.

Abigail looked up and at her surroundings as if to also scan for Eloise, when she saw something, or rather someone, she would very much like to unsee.

"Oh dear." She slipped out.

"What?" Anthony said, then stood up to turn and look where she was looking.

Lord Berbrooke was approaching, hot footed, clutching a piece of paper. As he got closer she winced at the sight of his purple and blue face.

"I bring cheerful news, Bridgertons!" He announced, rather too loudly. "I have taken matters into my own hands and sought a special license for my wedding to Miss Bridgerton."

"There is to be no wedding." Daphne said and approached the scene with the Duke behind her.

"I told you. The arrangement is canceled." Anthony said, clearly angry.

"Um Lord Berbrooke you look in a great deal of pain. Should we continue this conversation in a more private location?" Violet suggested from next to Abigail, trying to diffuse the situation.

"I require no further conversation. Though, perhaps I am finally speaking to the true head of the Bridgerton house. For if it were you," He looked toward Antony which for some reason made Abigail's insides twist in further anger. "I imagine you would have instructed your sister to take better care than to encourage certain attentions while alone with me on the dark walk at Vauxhall." This man just kept getting worse. "Of course, mère here say of such scandal could wreak havoc on even the most influential of families. What would someone like Lady Whistledown do, with such seemly information?" He was blatantly threatening them now.

"Is that a threat?" Anthony cut off, fuming.

"It is certainly not." He denied. Abigail scoffed. "Because in three days, I am to marry. I have the Diamond of the season. I have the very best the ton has to offer, I have a Bridgerton. And I shall save her, as well as your entire family, from the ruin which you could not protect them." He slammed the paper into Anthony's chest.

The Duke moved, or rather charged forward at the Lord, who flinched, but was held back by Benedict. Abigail looked between the two and made the connection that it must have been the Duke who had caused the unsightly blemishes on his face. She kept herself from smirking as it was much deserved.

"I look forward to the union of our great families." Lord Berbrooke finished his announcement with triumph. "Bridgerton. Miss Bentley." He acknowledged her with a look that made her want to throw up. "Hastings." Finally, he exited the tent.

Abigail watched him go but her gaze was caught by Daphne who looked as if she was about to keel over. Her breath was heavy and Abigail recognized the beginnings of a panic attack.

She swiftly moved forward and wrapped her friend in an embrace. Daphne reached to her and clung on as if her life depended on it. Abby could hear her wheezing and gripped her tighter in comfort.

"It'll be okay." She whispered."We can fix this."

Although, for as much as she wanted to believe it, she wasn't sure she did. Could they fix this? She knew one thing though. She was not going to let her best friend be subjected to a life with that man. At least not without a fight.

Chapter 8

Abigail ascended the steps leading up to the Bridgerton household, Olivia at her side. She was beginning to get quite used to the walk, in fact. Although, today she wished she could walk in with a brighter atmosphere around her. She knew Violet had her tea with The Queen that day, and she simply had to check on Daphne after the horrid end to the previous day.

The doors opened for her and she parted ways with Olivia. Walking towards the grand staircase she passed a particularly angry Bridgerton, wearing his top hat and coat, ready to go out. Although, in fairness, he always seemed to be irritated about something.

"I hope you aren't leaving to do anything idiotic." She said casually as they had just barely passed each other.

She heard him turn, so she did as well, just before she could reach the first step.

"Excuse me?" He questioned.

"For example, dueling would be categorized as idiotic." She continued on as if she didn't hear his question.

"I haven't said a word about dueling to you." He challenged.

"It's not hard to guess what you'd want to do in this situation." She sated, simply.

"Don't speak to me as if I am stupid."

"Stop acting like it, and I won't."

"You--"He must have had another insult in mind but he clearly stopped himself. "Why should you even care if I dueled Berbrooke?" He asked, more calmly this time. And quieter too, as he stepped closer.

After a moment's pause she repeated his own words back to him, "I care what happens to you."

He was taken aback by this, whether he should be or not was out of the question. He simply stood there, staring at her, recalling the time he said those exact words. They were in a very similar position then too. How did they always end up this close?

"Abigail?" They both heard the voice of Eloise question from upstairs.

Looking up, the both of them saw Eloise and Benedict at the top step of the stairs.

Taking a step back and a deep breath Abigail said, "Yes, hello Eloise!"

She made her way up the staircase herself, and passed Benedict on the way to meet his brother at the bottom. They nodded to acknowledge each other, and then Benedict focused his eyes solely on Anthony.

The two brothers made their way out of the house, before the younger of the two promptly smacked the elder on the back of his head.

"Ah! And what was that for?" Anthony questioned in a whine.

"What the hell are you doing, Brother?"

"What on God's green earth are you talking about?" He asked as he passed Benedict, and proceeded to walk down the street to their destination.

"Don't play dumb, Brother, it's beneath you." He moved to keep pace with Anthony. "Abigail."

Anthony kept his gaze forward, refusing to look his brother in the eye.

"I don't doubt you have some feelings for her." Benedict carried on. "But I know you are still running from the yoke because of that opera singer of yours. Abby doesn't have the time to wait for you. Why encourage her?"

"Sienna and I are done. I broke it off days ago." He stopped and spit the words of defense at his brother's accusation "And I would have you know I would never make a fool of the lady. I just-- I cannot always control what happens near her." He finally stuttered out.

Benedict paused for a moment before clapping his brother's shoulder.

"Well, you had better figure your life out soon. Because Abigail knows what she needs, and what she wants. Something tells me she won't put up with you if that means she cannot get it." And with that he placed his hat on his head and proceeded back on course, leaving Anthony staring at the concrete, unsure of his next move.

——

"Thank goodness you're here." Eloise said as she led Abigail down the hallway. "Daphne won't come out of her room. And I don't blame her, I just-- I could never make her feel better. We don't communicate well, and I'll say the wrong thing."

Abigail placed a hand on Eloise's shoulder as they approached Daphne's bedroom door.

"I've got this." She said, then glanced down at the book Eloise was carrying. She tapped it and said "That's quite good. I have the next in the series if you'd ever like to borrow it." Then she placed her hand on Daphne's doorknob and twisted.

Knocking on the door as she entered, she said softly, "It's just me."

"Oh Abby." Daphne said and got up from her chaise lounge. "I'm so grateful to see you." She hugged the Bentley woman tight.

"And I you." Abby replied and pulled back. "Daphne you really ought to get dressed." Noticing her nightdress and robe still on her body.

"What's the point?" She muttered.

"Perhaps a walk would make you feel better." Abigail said as cheerful as she could. "It really is quite lovely to-day." She moved over to Daphne's wardrobe and pulled out a drawer with her corsets and bloomers.

"I suppose it's worth a try." Daphne said and pulled on the cord next to her bed, calling for Rose to come and help her get dressed.

"Tell me something happy." Daphne requested and plopped on the bed.

Abigail arched her brow as she laid the undergarments on the bench.

"Well, I need something to take my mind off of... things."

"Alright then," Abby sat down on the bed next to Daphne. "Benjamin is supposed to be off to boarding school tomorrow. I've arranged for Calvin to go with him. Even though we typically would wait a year with him, I can't separate them. Not now."

"Rather smart." Daphne commented. "Do they offer Calvin's grade level?"

Abigail was about to reply when a knock came at the door.

"Come in Rose!" Daphne called.

Although, in fact, it was Violet who entered the room.

"Oh mama. How was your tea with The Queen?" Daphne asked.

"It was... educational." Violet said in reply. "I'm terribly sorry dear, but could I pull Abigail away for a moment."

"Oh. Of course."

Abby stood from the bed and exited the room right as Rose entered. Violet pulled her further down the hallway and then stopped in front of the study.

"Abigail, darling. Do you think you could join us for tea tomorrow afternoon?" She asked in a tone that said there was more to what she was actually asking.

"Um, of course." Abby replied, not knowing why she couldn't have asked this in front of Daphne.

"I think I've figured out a way to get the Baron off our hands." She said in explanation.

"Hopefully, the servants can get her lady's maid to talk about the Berbrooke family, so if your maid could help that'd be wonderful. Everyone knows the help hears everything, so why not use it to our advantage?"

Abigail smiled as she caught on, "And you're worried a tea with just you and Daphne might look abrupt?"

"Precisely. And by now, you're a part of this family yourself, so you should attend the tea."

Abigail's heart warmed. "I will be there."

"Excellent." Violet said and then walked off.

Abby's smile grew brighter as now they finally had a plan, and she turned around to make her way back towards Daphne's bedroom.

Chapter 9

♥

"Nigel is my one and only child." Lady Berbrooke rattled on. God in heaven, she sure could brag about her toad of a son.

Abigail sat at the tea table next to Daphne with a forced smile on her face. She knew this was necessary, and yet she couldn't help but think that if only the woman knew what her son was really like, she wouldn't boast so much.

"Very special boy, indeed. In fact, I often say God did not less me with another because perfection had already been achieved." She chuckled and bit into yet on ether cake.

"My goodness." Violet commented. Even she could see how awful that man was, and she didn't even know the full extent of his allegations.

"Mhm. Not every lady can be so blessed I know."

Abigail almost lunged across the table at her. That was a direct remark against Lady Bridgerton. Apparently condescension ran in the Berbrooke name.

"Miss Bridgerton..." Lady Berbrooke shifted the conversation and pulled Daphne out of her mind and back to the table. "Allow me to set my eyes upon you."

Abigail felt for her. Daphne didn't even know the purpose of this tea. As far as she knew she was still expected to marry this woman's odious son. And now, she was to be judged like a show dog in front of a woman who thought far too highly of herself.

"Certainly healthy, even if your countenance is a bit drawn." She remarked.

Abigail slyly reached over and grasped Daphne's hand in reassurance underneath the table. Some form of comfort she could provide.

"It was a terribly late evening." Violet came to her daughters defense.

She was rather impressive, how she was able to fake politeness in order to get done what was needed. Abby was unsure if she wanted to know how she had acquired this skill.

"All the excitement I suppose. Yet you must try harder, dear. My Nigel is quite discerning." Their guest continued to crow.

Abby snorted into her cup of tea, but quickly passed it off as a cough. Setting it down and continuing to clear her throat, she placed a hand on her chest and delicately smiled at the horrid woman in front of her, who glared suspiciously.

Although, she had made Daphne smile at least. A small one but still, she could see it out of the corner of her eye.

"He already turned away many more handsome debutantes," she cast a sidelong glance at Abigail who smiled, sickly sweet. "Saying 'Mother... I prize accomplishment over beauty.' Can you believe it?" She bit into the biscuit she was holding and it crunched loudly, filling the awkward silence in the room.

Abby noticed how much the stack of cookies had depleted since tea had started and she knew it solely had to do with the greedy woman in front of her.

"Shall I ring for some more biscuits?" She suggested and moved up from the tea table to pull the cord near the fireplace, alerting the servants hall downstairs.

"Miss Bentley..." Lady Berbrooke began as Abigail went to sit back down. "Tell me, what are you doing to find a match as superb as Miss Bridgerton and my Nigel's."

She didn't even have time to respond before Violet swooped in.

"Abigail is attending the season's events with us. I'm bringing her out with Daphne." Violet said.

"Well I would suppose you would have to after what happened to her mother." Lady Berbrooke commented which made Abigail's jaw set. "Tell me dear, the illness she died from, was that a familial trait?"

Abigail was too taken aback to say anything in response at first. All she could feel was anger. Direct fury she felt towards the woman. She would have acted on it too, if Mrs. Wilson hadn't come in with a fresh plate of biscuits at that moment. The housekeeper casted a mischievous glance at Lady Bridgerton as she set the plate down and politely exited the room.

Abigail took a deep breath. She just had to remember why she was enduring this. Olivia and Rose were gathering information as they spoke.

"No." She forced out with a pleasant look plastered on her face. "I don't believe it is."

"Good, you'll have an easier time finding a match if that isn't hanging over your head." Lady Berbrooke commented back.

"Lady Berbrooke, I don't believe we've seen you at any of the balls of the season yet." Violet changes subjects quickly and smoothly.

Abigail was glad she did so, for she was still frigid in her chair. She and Daphne exchanged strained glances, and Daphne gave her a look that seemed to be communicating the words, 'just breath'.

So Abigail took breath after breath, intermediately sipping her tea until the social exchange was finally over.

"Well I had really must be going." Lady Berbrooke stood, as did they all and Violet went to ring the servants. "You ate but not one bite at tea, my dear!" She moved to stand in front of Daphne. "A young lady must be well fed if she is to bear children. Kippers on rye every morning worked wonders for me when I conceived my Nigel."

Abby almost gagged but the maids entered then, interrupting them. Lady Berbrooke smiled and nodded towards herself and Lady Bridgerton, then took her maid with her as she left the room.   The second the footman closed the door Abigail turned and directed her attention towards the Lady' maids and Housekeeper.

"What have you found?" She asked immediately.

"What is going on?" Daphne asked from behind them.

"Well you could not think I would ask that woman for tea without a thought for you could you?" Violet turned and explained to Daphne. "The help hears everything, as we all know."

"She has heard a good deal in fact." Olivia started and then turned to Rose to finish.

"Lord Berbrooke has a boy by one of his maids that he refused to provide for." Rose revealed. "Sent the maid and child away to live off scraps."

Abigail covered her mouth with her hand, this is just what they needed.

"Horrible man." Mrs. Wilson added.

"Horrible enough for us to be rid of him, let us pray." Said Violet.

"Well, he- he will only deny it." Daphne began to pace and they all turned toward her. "And who will believe a group of women over a man's word?"

"Perhaps no one." Abigail started. "But they will if Lady Whistledown does." She smirked and turned towards Violet.

"Exactly, so we shall do what women do. We shall talk." She announced, and like that she was out of the room."

It has come to this author's attention that the ton is abuzz with a most sordid tale. It is said that one cannot judge a book by its cover. But in the case of the bumbling Baron Berbrooke, it seems his displeasing appearance is quite an apt metaphor for the state of affairs in his household. I would not be surprised if Lord Berbrooke were called away to the country on alleged Business. Business which, perhaps, might involve sending some much overdue funds to one former maid and young boy, who we can only hope takes after his mother.

Abigail read the gossip sheet mere days after their tea with the horrid Lady Berbrooke and immediately got up to visit the Bridgertons, and perhaps see how Daphne was feeling now that the problem seemed to be solved.

She smiled as the doors opened for her and she walked into the familiar foyer, gossip sheet in hand. Yet again, she saw Anthony descending the stairway. He too had a copy of Whistledown in hand.

He looked up as she proceeded forward and noticed the mischievous smile on her face. He didn't know what it was, instinct maybe, or the intense feeling that he knew her all that well. But, he immediately blocked her path and grabbed her wrist, pulling her into a door-frame.

"Did you do it?" He asked.

Abigail, who was still caught off guard said, "Excuse me?"

He held up his copy of Whistledown and she connected the dots. The copy was near her face, though in fairness so was he. They were rather close, which she wasn't sure if it had more to do with the low tones in which he wished to speak or... something else.

"I'm not inclined to think the solution to our problem has come about by chance." He spoke, again in a low volume.

Abby smiled slightly, although her heart was beating rather fast. Which, of course, she would never acknowledge.

"Why don't you ask your mother. It was her plan, I simply went along with it." She matched his volume. "Now if you'll excuse me, I'm going to check in on your sister."

She moved towards the staircase but her wrist was caught again by the Bridgerton before her, although this time more gently. She turned and looked back at him, the space between them still remaining the same, which was not much.

He wasn't sure why he'd stopped her this time. His hand just seemed to move, it didn't want her to go.

"Yes?" She prompted.

His breathing was just as heavy as her and he stared into her eyes, nearly getting lost in them.

"Nothing." He breathed out, consciously letting go of her.

She slowly backed away and finally turned to ascend the stairs. Both of their heads were muddled. Neither knew what to do with the unexplainable feelings stirring inside them.

Chapter 10

M usic played, soft and light. A wonderful juxtaposition of the movements her feet were making across the dance floor. Of course she wasn't alone. He was in front of her. His hand wrapped around her back holding her close to him as they waltzed in time to the dream-like music. The atmosphere was beautiful, twinkling lights and romantic trees set the scene. However, she couldn't seem to pull her eyes away from the man in front of her. He was captivating as he stared right back at her, as if he could see into her soul.

The next thing she knew they were alone on the dance floor. Although it had felt this way the whole time, now she had no choice but to be aware of the intimacy.

He twirled her outward, away from him. She felt free. Safe, and free. As she was starting to twirl back in she could feel his grip tighten around her bare hand. She continued to spin back towards him. When she landed back in front of him, her hands landed on his chest as his shot to her waist... then their lips met.

Abigail gasped and was jolted awake. She sat up and felt her night dress stick to her body due to the sweat she was covered in. Coming to terms with reality, she thought back to what caused her to wake so suddenly.

She had a dream. She had a dream of Anthony Bridgerton.

She sighed out only one word, "Damnit."

Abigail heard the Bridgerton family talking amongst themselves as she neared the parlor. She cautiously rounded the corner of the doorway, wanting to assess the situation before she interrupted anything.

She watched as Gregory stole a biscuit from Anthony's plate and he noticed only too late. He smiled and laughed, which made her smile herself. His expression was infectious like that. Without thinking she rounded the corner and leaned against the doorframe, continuing to gaze at him.

"And Lord Hardy is a fine option. Although he is rather boastful... Oh Abigail!" Daphne noticed her presence and the woman in question shifted her gaze as she was pulled from her thoughts.

Although as soon as her name was announced, she could practically feel his eyes watching her.

Was he thinking the same things as her? Did she ever inhabit his dreams? She pushed these intrusive thoughts to the side.

"I apologize for interrupting." She said, stepping further into the room, careful not to trod on Gregory and Hyacinth's building of blocks.

"Oh no please do." Eloise said from her slouched position on the armchair.

"I simply came to bring you this." She moved towards Eloise and handed her the book they had discussed.

She smiled and took the book, opening the cover, then her eyes went wide.

"Is this a first edition?" She questioned the Bentley.

"Yes." Abigail chuckled, careful to keep her eyes from drifting to the left, where the eldest Bridgerton sat.

Luckily she was soon distracted as arms were wrapped around her shoulders from a hug from Eloise. Abigail was taken aback but soon smiled and hugged the seventeen year old.

"Thank you." She said and pulled back, quickly opening it and exiting the room.

Abby's grin grew wider as she turned to watch her leave, happy she had made an impact. Then she heard Lady Bridgerton speak.

"My dear, you mustn't complicate matters. You must simply marry the man who feels like your dearest friend."

Abigail turned back the direction she was facing and finally made eye contact with Anthony. With a million thoughts running through her head and a million running through his, it'd be impossible to discern both, let alone one. Thankfully they were saved from trying as Daphne responded.

"Oh? Oh is that it, mama? Well, how very simple indeed!" Daphne said sarcastically.

Abby turned towards her and gave her a look. In which Daphne responded with an irritated shrug. Narrowing her eyes, she guessed that the Duke was starting to feel like Daphne's dearest friend. But she knew her friend would never admit it so she decided not to press.

"Well, I should be going." She announced and made a move to leave the room.

"Oh nonsense, darling, why don't you stay and have some tea? Daphne says your brother have left for school so I can't imagine you're eager to get home." Violet said, with empathy in her tone.

"Uh, yes they have." She said and moved to sit next to her. She tried not to sound too sad, she knew how good it was for them to be out of the house. "I quite miss them if that doesn't sound too feeble. It's nowhere near as fun in the house with just Father and I."

"Ah yes, how is your father? I don't see him at anything nowadays." Benedict questioned from the couch across her

'Probably because I don't want him out of the house.' She thought, but thankfully didn't say out loud.

"He... he isn't one for balls." She danced around the question. "And he's always been a terrible betting man, so I doubt you'd see him at any clubs."

Anthony watched as she smiled and laughed around the question. Something struck him as odd. He didn't mean to pretend he knew her so well, but he couldn't deny the connection they felt.

And whilst the connection would normally make his chest tighten or his head spin, at the moment it was telling him that something was off. She wasn't telling the whole truth. He couldn't explain why he cared, but he did. And whatever was going on, he was sure he'd find out.

Chapter 11

♥

The string quartet played a playful yet suspenseful tune as the guests danced in the middle of the floor. The room was lined with peacocks and exotic birds, some alive, some not. Nevertheless, the room burst with color and laughter.

Anthony, however, was lost in his own head. He wasn't distracted by the atmosphere around him, no. He was much too focused on his thoughts, as well as the woman that consumed them.

Abigail was, at the moment, distracted by Lord Tomkins as he seemed to be writing his name on the appropriate line of her dance card. Anthony could feel a twinge of jealousy as he watched the two interact, but he was mostly consumed with the need to know her. Know why she lied, why she avoids questions about her father. He was nearly sure he knew why, he just needed it confirmed.

So, he took matters into his own hands and swept across the room only to land in front of her. Lord Tomkins had just left her. Probably to scour for other young ladies to dance with, he thought bitterly.

"I hope that dance card isn't too full." He said, making her turn as he gained her attention.

"As a matter of fact, there's one space left, if you're interested." She quirked her brow, and held out the card in question.

"A quadrille? Alright, but I'm not promising anything." He chuckled as he signed his name.

"Oh he's losing steam. I thought a Bridgerton, of all people, would have had every dance on this list down to perfection." She decided to tease him.

Her smile was infectious to him. He matched her expression.

"We're supposed to. But um," He leaned down to her ear and lowered his voice. "I may have ditched a few dance classes when it was my turn."

She laughed and chose to ignore the way her heart skipped a beat when he came nearer to her.

"Miss Bentley." She heard from behind her. Turning she saw Lord Ainsworth, who had cornered her for a dance almost as soon as she walked in the door. "I do believe this is the Redowa. If you'll allow me to take her from you, Lord Bridgerton."

Anthony pushed down his irritation and said, "Of course."

Abby spared him one last glance before leaving his side and entering the dance floor. She didn't want to feel anything for him, but she couldn't help feeling a sense of anticipation for his dance. She shouldn't. She knew full well he wasn't planning on marrying anytime soon, and she also knew she didn't have time to wait for him. But lately, whatever was between them seemed to be growing stronger. By the way he was acting, she didn't even think he could deny it.

Time however went quickly and soon enough, she didn't have time to question the multitude of thoughts over him, for he was in front of her, ready for his turn.

"Alright. Remember what I said about not expecting too much." He said quietly as the music started up.

They started moving.

"Just don't trod on my toes."

He laughed at that. It was refreshing, he couldn't remember the last time he felt this at ease with someone.

They danced in comfortable silence for a few moments, until he finally broke it.

"May I ask you a question?"

"You just did." She smirked and he rolled his eyes, as he was used to this response having the amount of siblings he does. "But go ahead."

"What really happened to your cheek the other day?" He asked in a low tone.

That, she was not expecting. All ease displayed on her face was gone.

"I-I told you." She managed out.

"No, you didn't. You avoided the question." He responded, as if he had been ready for her answer. "You seem to skillfully avoid every question about your home life, when it doesn't have to do with your brothers."

She was utterly flustered, and avoided eye contact with him. Instead, she focused on the music, and when it might soon end.

"Abigail." He gained her attention. "Did your father hurt you?"

Now she was not only flustered but also thoroughly irritated. Thankfully the song ended. She removed herself from his grasp immediately, and swiftly left the ballroom, attempting not to gain too much attention.

He sighed, frustrated, and went after her. He followed her into the hallway where she was already charging down a corridor. She made a right, so he made a right.

"Abigail!" He yelled, but barely above a whisper. They shouldn't be alone out here. "Stop walking."

"Stop following." She forcefully said back.

He managed to grab her wrist, effectively stopping her, and turned her to face him. She, however, released herself from his grasp, still fuming.

"You know what your problem is?" She started, not waiting for an answer. "You have this idea that if something is wrong, you can fix it. Guess what? You can't. You have no idea what the world is like for me."

"Abigail, if your father is hurting you in some way I can help." He insisted. She scoffed. "I can report him. Get you out of there."

She stepped forward, angry.

"And what would that do to my reputation? My family's? I need to find a husband willing to take care of me and my brothers. If the ton knew he was a drunk, incapable of functioning-- me, not to mention both my brothers, would be ruined." She explained, her tone harsh but her volume low.

"You cannot fix this. I am not some damsel in need of saving. I can handle—"

But her words were cut off as he suddenly pulled her close and his lips crashed on hers. His hand snaking round her waist and hers instinctually moving to tangle in his hair.

Chapter 12

They were entwined with each other. Neither willing to let go of the other, they pulled closer and closer, hoping to melt into one another.

She pulled harder on the back of his neck, willing him to be closer. She could feel his lips on her own. Hot and kissing her fiercely as if they had wanted to for so long, but couldn't. It was almost as if they were both desperate; desperate to feel all of each other.

He gripped her waist as if his life depended on it. His hands moved, as if on their own, up to the buttons that clasped her dress together. Managing a couple loose.

He would have managed more too, if it hadn't been for the fist around the neck of his jacket, forcefully pulling him back and away from her.

"Are you insane?!" It was Benedict.

Abigail, shocked at first for the abrupt stop, breathed a sigh of relief as she recognized it was him, and no one who would make trouble. Then again, she was breathing rather hard in the first place, so she wasn't sure if it was a sigh of relief or just simply an attempt to catch her breath.

"What are you doing out here?" Anthony questioned his brother.

"Are we honestly questioning my whereabouts right now?" His voice was barely above a whisper, but he spoke as if he was capable of screaming. "What the hell were you thinking?"

"I wasn't." Anthony continued to argue with his brother, though Abigail had a suspicion he was redirecting other emotions. "But you have no right to lecture me."

"I have every right if you are going to drag Abigail—"

"Enough!" She spoke over them, exasperated. "Honestly, you two speak as if I had no choice in the matter." She muttered that part more to herself.

She huffed a frustrated sigh.

"From what I can tell, we weren't seen. So we can all stop talking about it." She began to turn, ending everything abruptly. With a last glance at him from over her shoulder she said, "You two stay for a moment." And with that, she left.

She didn't take a moment to talk to him. She didn't insist they be left alone. She left. Abigail wasn't sure if this was the right choice, but this was the choice that was being made, and it was certainly too late to change it.

After all, Anthony didn't want to get married. He certainly didn't want to talk about any feelings they might have for each other. Right?

Abigail entered the ballroom, finally, after a walk down what felt like the longest corridor in the world. She could hear some commotion happening, but she was still mostly in her head. So she spotted Daphne standing next to The Duke and headed their way.

"—to my book I shall know who to ask." She heard Daphne finish

"What is happening?" She landed next to Daphne.

"Oh," Daphne turned in her direction. "The Prince is here. Where have you been?"

"Ladies room." She lied with ease.

"Oh, I do believe he just told Miss Cowper that her gown is exquisite." Simon made a comment. Clearly, carrying on a previous conversation, but Abby laughed anyway.

"Do you think so?" Daphne laughed.

"He is here to tell every lady the very same thing." Simon said before he had to move to make way for his Highness and her Majesty.

"Prince Friedrich, these are the young ladies I was telling you about. Miss Bridgerton, the season's diamond; and Miss Bentley, the incomparable." The Queen boasted.

Both ladies curtsied when their name was said. The Prince reached for Daphne's hand first, and kissed it.

"So lovely to meet you Miss Bridgerton. Your gown, it is exquisite."

At that moment both ladies burst out laughing. Abigail became quite flushed because she knew they shouldn't be, but she simply couldn't seem to stop. Unfortunately Daphne's only worsened as she managed to let out a snort, which only made the two ladies laugh harder.

"Oh, oh we do apologize, your highness." Daphne said almost immediately.

"Yes, I'm truly sorry." Abigail was still chuckling, desperately trying to calm down.

"No apologies necessary." He played off, smoothly.

"Perhaps a small one." The Queen commented and attempted to guide her nephew away.

But the Prince stopped her, and very intentionally reached for Abigail's hand and kissed it.

"It was lovely to meet you." He said softly before walking away with his aunt.

Abigail smiled, and blushed despite herself. As she let her hand drop, she caught Anthony's eye from across the room. Evidently as far away from her as he could get. She must have missed his re-entrance, for he and

Benedict now stood side by side against a wall. Benedict was not attempting to hide his glare.

But she wasn't distracted by him, she was distracted by Anthony who did not remove his gaze from hers. She wished she could read him for she couldn't tell anything that was happening in his head.

Chapter 13

Anthony felt the dice rattling in his hands and could feel the effects of the alcohol he had liberally imbibed upon entering his club. He needed this, a distraction.

"Here we go, here we go. Come on." He wished aloud as he rolled the dice from his hands.

They were in his favor. All the men who had crowded around it laughed and cheered.

"Me again." He announced.

"Indeed. I am inclined to investigate the providence of such lucky dice." Lord Featherington commented with bitterness in his tone.

"Did they not land the same way when you were casting, Featherington? Perhaps the common element is you. Might it be best to show some restraint?" Simon came to Anthony's defense.

"Restraint, I fear, is not among Lord Featherington's skills." Anthony laughed as he walked away with his money.

"I seem to have done it, Bridgerton." Simon followed him.

"Done what?" He made his way towards the chairs.

"Proved you remain capable of laughing again in my presence."

"You cannot fault me for being doubtful of your intentions."

Simon downed the rest of his drink, then said, "Indeed I can. For all the mischief you have witnessed me make, you would also have known I would never make a fool of a lady, and certainly not one such as your sister."

Anthony sat down and eyed him, thinking of how he might have made a fool of one himself.

"You confound me. You are respectful, and yet I know you have no intention of marriage. Has that changed?"

"I cannot claim so." Simon replied.

"Then whatever could your intentions be?" He fired the question as if from a gun.

"Respectful. Might we leave it there?" Simon ended the conversation. "What about you? You still running from the yoke?" He shifted the attention off of him.

"That is a more complicated matter." Anthony moved to pour more brandy.

"Aha! I knew there was something with the Bentley girl." The Duke smiled into his own glass.

"How did you--?" He turned to look at his friend in confusion.

"Oh please, Bridgerton, you've always been a terrible secret keeper." He clapped his shoulder. "But if you care for her then you have my congratulations."

"Well, as I said, it is more complicated than that." He took a large swig from his glass.

"But you do care for her?"

Antony thought for a moment, but it didn't take long for him to answer with finality.

"Yes, yes I do."

Just then, the doors to the club opened and several women of the night entered to whistles and cheers. Amongst them was a face Anthony recognized: Sienna. What was strange is that he thought he would have felt more. Maybe jealousy or anger at her appearance. But he didn't. If anything he felt that it was simply a sign he should go home.

He excused himself from the Duke's company and left, headed back to his family home to complete the bookings he had started earlier that evening.

He made it there in almost no time and had just set his jacket on a chair inside his father's study when he heard the floorboards creak in the hallway. This was strange, considering no servants should be up at this time. He left the study and spotted Daphne exiting her bedroom and heading for the stairs.

"Sister? Whatever are you doing?" He interrupted.

He appeared to have startled her for she breathed a sigh of relief when she turned and him.

"I could not sleep. I thought a bit of warm milk might help matters." She explained.

"Well should I ring for a servant?" He suggested.

"No. No, do not wake them." She paused for a minute, then asked, "would you like to join me?"

Surprised at this, since he thought she wasn't too happy with him, he agreed and they made their way down to the kitchen. Once there, they procured the milk from the icebox and stood in front of the stove.

Both seemed to be waiting for the other. In truth, neither knew the workings of the contraption.

"Well we should light it." Daphne suggested.

"Excellent idea." He agreed.

"Well... go on." She coaxed.

"Me?"

"Well I should not know how to do it."

"And you believe I should?"

Several more moments passed of them simply staring at the stove.

Finally, Daphne suggested, "Cold milk then."

"Most refreshing given the heat." Anthony recovered.

She passed him a jar and he took a swig as they sat on counters opposite each other.

"Can I ask you a question, Brother?" She began.

"So long as it has nothing to do with the inner workings of... that thing." He chuckled.

"Two questions actually. The first is a question about Abigail."

"Oh not you too, Daph." He groaned.

"I can see you care for her. And not to be protective, but the last I checked you weren't ever planning on marrying. So, has that changed or are you simply having her on?" She questioned, seriously.

"No. I am not." He answered almost immediately. "I... I would never make a fool of her. I just, I cannot read her mind and there is simply a communication blockage at the moment... I hope." He muttered the last part more to himself.

"How did you even know?" He asked out of curiosity.

"You two are not subtle about your glances across the ballroom. And I'd like to think I'm not stupid." She added.

"You certainly are not." He laughed. "What was your second question?"

She hesitated for a moment then said, "It is about the Duke."

Anthony let out a long sigh, he had a feeling this was going to be a slightly more awkward conversation.

Chapter 14

♥

Whenever the whole Bridgerton family is leaving for an event, it is bound to be chaotic, and this occasion was no exception. As Gregory and Hyacinth bounded through the downstairs foyer, nannies in toe, the rest of the ladies were attempting to make their way downstairs with maids fussing about either their hair or their belongings. The Bridgerton boys, however, were already in the foyer, ready to go. Anthony and Benedict stood on opposite sides of the room, using much effort not to make eye contact. Colin paced back and forth excitedly, holding his top hat in one hand and Whistledown in the other.

"Here we all are." Violet anounced as they finally descended the steps. "Gregory! Hyacinth! Let us go now!" They all began to make their way to the door.

"Mother? Is Abigail not coming today?" Anthony questioned, noticing she did not descend the steps with them.

"Of course she is dear, she is meeting us there. Why?" Violet turned around just before exiting through the doors.

"I just- She just usually arrives with us for these things that is all." Anthony said, rather flustered.

Daphne snorted as she passed him and he elbowed her on the way out.

"Don't." He whispered as he led her to the carriage.

"I said nothing." She whispered back, then took his hand to stabilize herself upon entering the carriage.

The ride was not long and soon enough they had all arrived at Somerset House. The youngest Bridgertons bounded out of their carriages and had to be called back in by their mother. Anthony offered his arm to her and they began to walk behind the rest of the family, partly to keep an eye on the two in front.

As they walked into the grand home, Anthony's eyes scanned the group of young ladies that surrounded the Prince, hoping to spot Abigail. He did not quite realize he was doing it until he concluded she wasn't there, then felt a sense of disappointment. It had seemed they had arrived before her.

Walking into the grand room of paintings was certainly a sight, indeed. However, Anthony didn't get to enjoy it long before his mothers voice interrupted his thoughts.

"Miss Anna Vaughn. Speaks several languages, I hear." She commented, pointing out the lady in question. "Miss Mary Egglesfield. She's meant to be quite the reader."

"Were I looking for a list of debutantes and their dubious accomplishments, I could have stayed home and read Lady Whistledown." He cut her off before walking away from her, swiftly. There was only one debutante that occupied his mind, and she had yet to arrive.

Although, without his knowledge, she had arrived. She slipped in, so no one would notice her lack of escort, and quickly scanned the room. Spotting Anthony, she intentionally walked in the opposite direction. Landing, in fact, next to Benedict.

"You do not seem pleased with the painting before you." She noted, gaining his attention.

"Ah, I see you've arrived." He greeted her. "And you would be correct. It's much too cold." He began dissecting it as Lady Danbury and a man Abigail did not know arrived on his other side. "Where's any sense of the subject's spirit? And the light! Given the quality, I do wonder why the piece was not skied with the other daubs."

"Perhaps we should as the artist." Lady Danbury pointed out.

Abigail could sense there was something up her sleeve. Did she know the artist?

"Well that would be something, Lady Danbury." Benedict said, sarcastically.

"Mm... Mr. Granville, why was your piece not skied?" She turned to the man on her right, and asked.

Abigail immediately snorted, and her hand flew to her mouth as she suppressed her laughter.

"Mr. Granville, I—"

"If you will excuse me, I must find my wife." He excuse himself as Benedict sputtered.

"You diabolical... How could you let me rattle on like that?" He questioned Lady Danbury.

"How could I not my dear Mr. Bridgerton? It was riotously funny, you must admit." And with that, she walked away.

"Don't." Benedict simply said as Abigail failed to further suppress her laughter.

"I am saying nothing." She held her hands up in mock defense.

"Well, keep it that way."

A few moments passed between them as Abigail regained control of her laughter and they simply moved to look at another painting.

"I..." He started but then trailed off.

"Yes?" She prompted, continuing to stare ahead at the painting.

"I must apologize for my brother." He referred to the other night.

Abby blushed involuntarily.

"You should do no such thing. I certainly didn't fight it, in fact... I think part of me wished for it to happen." Her sentence got quieter at the end.

A few moments passed between them before Benedict spoke again.

"May I ask something that might be considered improper?"

"I think you've earned it." She said in response.

"Do you wish to marry my brother?" He asked.

Taken aback by this, she said, "It does not matter what I wish. Your brother has made it quite clear he intends not to marry."

Benedict sighed and said, "That may have been true, but now he seems to wish to marry you. Or at least court you I certainly cannot speak for—"

"What?" She cut him off in astonishment.

"I was simply saying that I cannot speak for him but—"

"Would you excuse me?" She requested, but did not wait for his reply before she charged off into the crowd.

Now, far from avoiding him, she was looking for him. She worked her way through the room, and when that ended in no avail, she landed in the foyer that was also chalked full of paintings. Sighing, she turned around, and that's when her eyes finally landed on him.

He must have felt her gaze, for mere moments after she her eyes found him, his eyes found hers. She wasn't quite sure how but he managed to take her breath away very time he looked at her that way he did.

She took a step to move toward him. As did he, but they had each only managed a few before a voice calling her name interrupted her movements.

"Miss Bentley!" It was the Prince who had called her, and now he had landed right in front of her.

"Oh, your highness." She acknowledged him in politeness, and curtsied.

"I was hoping to see you today." He said with his accent lilting his words.

"Were you?" She was still a little flustered from being interrupted moments before.

"Yes, it seems the art is not the only beautiful thing on display, at present." He payed her a compliment and she smiled.

"Um, tell me you must have traveled widely. How do you find London compared to elsewhere?" She asked, politely.

"It is one of my favorite cities. Have you travelled much? I think you would just love the music of Vienna." He asked.

However, what he asked went unnoticed by her, because when she glanced over, Anthony was no longer in the spot he just was. Because she had completely missed what he said, she simply made an excuse.

"If you will excuse me for one moment, I am being summoned." She then delved back into the crowd and left the Prince without another thought.

Yet, she searched and searched and Anthony was nowhere to be found. It seemed that during her conversation with the Prince, he had simply disappeared.

Chapter 15

Abigail walked up the familiar steps of the Bridgerton household, immediately parting ways with Olivia once inside. One would think she'd be used to it by now, and to a certain level she was, but as a footman escorted her upstairs she couldn't deny the sense of warmth she enjoyed feeling every time she entered the house.

She was here under the guise of paying Daphne a visit, but really, she was looking for Anthony. It had been almost four days since the gallery showing at Somerset house and she had yet to see him at any social function. Impatient with waiting, she decided this morning to go straight to the source.

The footman dropped her off at the drawing room, and she nodded to him that she was fine to be left there. She didn't stay, however. Once she was sure the footman had left, she exited the drawing room and proceeded to search for his study down the hallway. It wasn't difficult to locate, the large doors were open and she could see him scribbling away with his quill.

She had to catch herself not to simply stand in the doorway and stare. She entered the room and lightly knocked on the open door next to her, to announce her presence. He looked up, and for a moment, she could make out a sense of shock on his face, but he recovered it quickly.

"Have you, um, seen your sister?" She asked, attempting to start the conversation.

"You will have to be more specific," He said in an oddly cold tone. "I have quite a few."

"Daphne." She simply responded, taken aback by his lack of warmth or essentially any emotion at all.

"Last I heard, she went to the modiste with mother." He replied, simply, then turned his head downward and back toward his books.

"Ah, I see..." she trailed off.

She wasn't sure what she should do. Sure, she had just been informed that the person she came to see wasn't here, but the person she had really come to see was sitting right in front of her, acting as cold as ever. She made to leave, but lingered, staring at him in confusion.

"Is there anything else?" He didn't even look up from his writing at this time.

"Is there—" she started to repeat back in astonishment. "You left rather abruptly at Somerset." She changed courses, trying to get to the real point.

"Yes well, loads to do." He stood and closed his book, apparently packing up his things. "Unlike others my life isn't all attending parties and charming men."

That was low. Something else was going on with him. Even if Anthony was mad at her, he normally would retain a certain level of class. Something was bothering him.

With his breifcase in hand, he moved to pass her and exit the room. But before he could do so, her arm reached out, almost of its own accord and blocked his path.

"You are blocking my way." He stated, looking at her but somehow avoiding her eyes.

"Yes," she started, harshly. "Believe it or not that was my intention."

"Well, what is it?" He still wasn't making eye contact with her.

"What is it?" She repeated back angrily, her hand still blocking his path on the doorframe. "I tried to talk to you at the gallery and, correct me if I'm wrong, it seemed as if you wanted to talk to me as well."

"Yes, well— that was then." He said too quickly, and made to move again.

This time, not only was her arm there, but she stopped her body in front of him as well.

"Oh no, you will not leave through this door until you talk to me, or at least look me in the eye." She said, stubbornly.

It took him a moment but finally, he looked up and into her eyes. He seemed to be having a sort of internal battle, but she couldn't tell with what.

"If you recall..." He was not having an easy time forming words as he maintained eye contact with her. "That almost-conversation was interrupted by the Prince. I, I could never— I would never want to stop you from such an advantageous marriage. You have made it clear you need this, and I wouldn't dream of stopping you from such things." He finally ducked his head at the last sentence.

That's when everything clicked. He was trying to help, in his own, somewhat irritating way. But he didn't understand, she had to make that clear to him.

"What I need... I don't care about the prince. He's very nice, and would make a wonderful husband, I'm sure. But not to me. I- I don't want--" she fumbled with her own words.

But it didn't matter, for mere moments after she began to stutter, his lips were on hers. It didn't take much for him to give in to this desire, for he'd been wanting to for several days now.

His book bag dropped and his arms wrapped around her waist, gleefully picking her up from the floor and spinning her around. She smiled into the kiss as she clung onto his shoulders for balance. He set her back on the floor and they broke apart.

"I want to marry you, Abiagil." He said almost immediately. "I never thought I'd say that but it's true."

She laughed and cupped his cheek with her hand to pull him into another kiss. And just like that, they were wrapped in another embrace.

He pulled apart again, "Can I take that as a yes?"

"In every language." She smiled, broadly.

He was about to say something, when they both heard the voice of his sister making her way down the hall.

"Abigail?" She called.

Abby stole one quick kiss from Anthony before whispering, "We'll discuss this later."

She swiftly exited the study and found Daphne facing the opposite direction as her, making her way down the hall.

"I'm here." She stated.

Her friend turned around and Abigail noted the determined look on her face.

"Ah, Mrs. Wilson said you were here." She walked forward and grabbed Abby's hand to pull her into her room. "Come, I must ask you something."

Once in Daphne's bedroom, she pulled Abby to the bench at the end of the bed and looked her in the eye.

"Alright, I know the Prince has shown interest in you as well." Daphne began. "I was just wondering if your intentions were serious with him."

Abigail blushed, thinking back to moments before with Anthony.

"No, no they are not."

Daphne looked relieved, the mischievous glint appeared back in her eye. Abby raised an eyebrow, apprehensively.

"Alright then, I need your help."

She was up to something, but nothing that Abigail could guess. She did, though, had a feeling this would be an interesting ride.

Chapter 16

♥

Abigail sat in the Bridgerton family drawing room, talking with Eloise about the book she had lent her. Hyacinth and Gregory sat playing a card game across from them, and Anthony sat at the table and chairs reading his paper and discussing it with Colin.

They all were, of course, waiting for Daphne and Lady Bridgerton to return from their afternoon soirée at court.

Last night, Daphne had explained everything to Abigail. The Duke's abrupt end to their deal, and then her plan to now court the Prince. Abby could see her friend was in pain and guessed she had some very real feelings for the Duke, despite what she insisted, but she decided to let her find this out for herself. For now, she would simply support her friend and help her find an advantageous match. So, last night she watched her openly flirt and dance with the Prince. She also watched the Duke leave the ballroom, obviously hurt, but she had a feeling this might have been Daphne's intention.

Now, she waited for Daphne to return, per her request. Hyacinth seemed to be bouncing on the floor with anticipation for her sister's arrival. However, she was the only one apparently who displayed their excitement. For everyone else seemed to be going about with their business as usual.

"Is Daphne coming back soon?" Hyacinth asked for what appeared to be the thousandth time.

Abigail heard Eloise groan next to her. Knowing she was about to snap, she decided to intervene.

"Soon." Abby assured. "Time will go by faster if you think of something else until then."

"But how do I do that?" Hyacinth whined.

At this, Abigail blushed, for she hadn't seemed to have any trouble passing the time. She and Anthony had been exchanging glances across the room for almost the past hour. Sure, she was talking to Eloise but she could practically feel him watching her. Anytime she looked up, his eyes were already on her.

Realizing she hadn't responded the question she shook herself from her thoughts, and was about to reply when Gregory tapped Hyacinth on the shoulder yelling, "Tag! You're it!" And he ran off with her in toe.

"Ugh, there are times when I want to shut her in a closet." Eloise said and turned her attention back to the conversation they were having.

However, yet again, Abigail had trouble focusing for she could feel him watching her. When she looked up he was smirking, then turned his attention back to his newspaper.

"...anyway, what have you been reading lately, Abby?" Eloise finished her sentence, the first half of which Abigail didn't catch at all.

She turned her head and gave a quick answer, "Hm? Oh, um Sense and Sensibility was a recent one. If you'll excuse me, I must powder my nose." She made the excuse and quickly stood up, locking eyes with Anthony before she left the room.

She made her way down the hallway and veered the opposite direction of the powder room, instead, making her way to the study. Walking in she decided to wait, and see if he figured out her signal. She wandered about the room and her eyes caught on the portrait of Lord Bridgerton, Anthony's father, above the mantel. She was just noticing the likeness between him and his sons when she felt her arm being tugged and she was quickly spun around.

In practically no time Anthony's lips were on hers and she smiled into it as she wrapped her arms over his shoulders. His found her waist and it felt so nice and automatic.

She tried to pull away, but he didn't seem to want to let her as he pulled on her back and kissed her harder. She chuckled as she experienced what she could only assume was pure bliss.

She tried pulling back slightly again and was more successful this time as she got a couple of words in.

"So I've been thinking." She started.

"Mhm." He acknowledged, reconnecting their lips.

She smiled and this time actually pulled back, placing her hands on his chest so as to keep him there.

"I think we should wait a bit longer, to announce every-thing." She said.

His brow furrowed.

"Don't misunderstand me, this sneaking around is great fun," He smiled and placed a kiss on her neck. "But it is a miracle we haven't been caught already."

"Listen," She sighed. "Your mother is very preoccupied with Daphne right now. And Daphne, has just had her heart broken, no matter how much she doesn't want to admit it."

"This is all very well, but I would like to kiss you in public one day. Do try to work that into your overly empathetic brain, please." He said in what she knew was seriousness whether he masked it with sarcasm or not.

Nevertheless, she laughed and threw her head back slightly. He took the opportunity to swoop in and begin kissing her neck. Soon, her breathing turned heavy and she pulled his face up to meet hers. He responded with enthusiasm and she knew it was going to be very hard to stop if they went any further.

Luckily, the excuse came quickly as they heard the front door open and Hyacinth's voice began to pester Daphne with questions. Finally, Abby pulled away from the kiss and swiftly backed away to exit the room. She heard him groan and she turned around to wink at him before exiting the room.

She ran slightly to catch up with Daphne at her bedroom door. There, Hyacinth stood, asking question after question as Daphne attempted to shut the door.

"Hyacinth, your governess was calling for you." She called and distracted her.

The youngest Bridgerton ran off and Abigail took in Daphne's appearance. She was now wearing the largest diamond necklace Abby had ever seen, but she also appeared to be hyperventilating. Abby quickly pushed her into the bedroom and just managed to catch her as Daphne nearly collapsed against the wall.

This was about to get very complicated.

Chapter 17

Abigail entered the Trowbridge ball side by side with the rest of the Bridgertons. Benedict, once again escorting her on his arm as Anthony led his sister in, and Colin led his mother. Just like Daphne and Violet, she too wore a black band around her deep, blush pink dress and a black flower in her hair, holding up her half updo.

The ballroom was alight with dancers and trapeze artists hanging from the ceiling. Taking in the scenery, Abby could see what Lady Whistledown meant by referencing the 'sensual nature' of the ball.

She watched Daphne walk off with Anthony; and Colin leave to, she assumed, find Miss Thompson. That left her with Benedict and Violet.

"Abigail, why don't you come and keep me company for a moment." Violet beckoned for her and she exchanged a glance with Benedict so as to apologize for leaving him.

She walked over and stood next to Lady Bridgerton, who almost immediately reached for two champagne flutes. One she handed to Abigail, the other she practically downed in one gulp.

Abby smirked into her own flute as she fallowed the woman's gaze and saw she was watching Daphne greet the Prince. She knew her children were driving her insane and, of course, she felt for her, but at the moment she was simply finding it a little funny.

Anthony joined herself and his mother soon enough, and Violet seemed to wave someone over.

"Ah good, Anthony. This is Miss Addington, the Earl of Lindsay's niece." Violet pulled the young lady she had called over and introduced her to her son.

"Pleasure." Anthony greeted.

She wasn't sure if he could, but Abigail could see exactly what was going on. She clenched her glass and felt a strange tightening sensation in her stomach which she could only assume to be identified as jealousy.

"See?" Violet said to Miss Addington. "Perhaps you two could..." then she trailed off, expecting him to know she meant dance.

"I would love to," he started and Abigail felt the pit in her stomach grow tighter. "But unfortunately I came over here to ask Miss Bentley to dance." He said and reached for her hand, clearly quick to get out of the situation.

She accepted it and set her champagne on a passing tray as he pulled her out onto the dance floor. They began a waltz.

"I would object to that being terribly rude, but I have to say, I'm rather glad you did it." She said in a low volume as the swept across the floor.

He smirked at this and said, "Is that jealousy I detect, Miss Bentley?"

Knowing she couldn't deny it, she simply said, "It might be."

She saw his smirk grow wider and began to defend herself but she was cut off by a question he asked.

"How scandalous you think it would be if we left to take a walk?"

She was suddenly very flustered with the openness of his flirting and took a moment before she replied.

"Well, technically we're not supposed to be alone together."

"Oh yes, because we have followed the rules very closely till now." He said, sarcastically, at which she laughed.

She hesitated another moment before finally saying, "Alright, what's life without some risk?"

"My thoughts exactly." He whispered in her ear and then stepped back to bow as the music was ending.

"Meet you on the terrace." He whispered after she curtsied, and he parted ways with her.

Her breathing now was rather heavy as there was a lot more risk involved in this interaction. She slowly and casually made her way to the terrace. Once there, she looked behind her to make sure no one in the ballroom had a clear view of her, and she leaned against the railing to look up at the stars.

A throat cleared next to her and she jumped slightly but only turned to see Anthony leaning his body sideways against the wall of the building.

"I thought a walk." He simply said and reached for her hand.

She smiled, then hesitated before finally taking it and letting him lead her down the steps to the maze.

She linked arms with him and enjoyed the quiet as they strode along the path.

"Is this all you wanted?" She questioned. "Peace and quiet?"

"And your company." He added. "Something I'm eager to enjoy in public." He hinted, not so subtly.

"Soon I promise, I—"but she cut herself off as she heard voices near them.

She looked in the direction of them, and then back at Anthony. He heard them too, and he motioned for her to stay as he walked ahead to the archway on the right. He stopped, and she watched as his face twisted to one of horror, then rage.

"Bastard!" He screamed, and ran forward, out of her view.

She heard a punch and a grunt of pain, and ran forward herself.

"Anthony!" Daphne exclaimed as Abigail arrived on scene to see him standing over the Duke, punching him in the face.

Daphne turned and locked eyes with Abigail. She ran toward her, gripping her arms and watched the scene before them.

"You will marry her." Anthony said as he stood up, obviously finished with beating him.

"What?" Daphne questioned, obviously in shock.

Neither of the men heard her, or at least they didn't acknowledge her.

"Immediately." He carried on as if she hadn't spoken. "We can only hope no one saw you take such liberties, and that my sister is saved further mortification. You will marry her!" He was a seething kind of angry at this point.

"Brother!" Daphne tried to interject once again but was, again, interrupted. This time by the Duke.

"I cannot marry her." He said in a low, almost sorrowful tone.

Abigail felt Daphne's grip on her arm tighten.

"You have defiled her innocence, and now you refuse her hand?" Anthony questioned in disbelief.

In complete honesty, Abigail was growing irritated with him, as he continued to speak as if Daphne wasn't there, without any choice in the matter.

The Duke sighed and looked down, avoiding anyone's gaze, but Anthony didn't allow him to as he walked forward.

"I knew you were a rake, Hastings, I never thought you a villain."

"I cannot marry her." The Duke repeated, this time looking up, apparently refusing Daphne's gaze.

Abigail watched as Daphne's face continued to fall with sadness and hurt.

"Then you leave me no choice." Anthony announced. "I must demand satisfaction."

She knew what that meant, and she could feel her heart drop to the depths of her stomach. She couldn't stay an observer any longer.

"A duel? Anthony, you cannot—" Abby began to insist.

"He dishonors my sister!" He explained, forcefully. Then, turned to his sister. "He dishonors you, and me and the very Bridgerton name. I have misjudged you, indeed." He now turned toward the Duke. "You have duped us both, but I shall not see my sister pay for my own misdeeds. We will settle this as gentlemen!"

"I understand." The Duke said, a little too calmly. "I shall see you at dawn."

Daphne finally spoke to the Duke.

"I do not understand. You would rather die than marry me?" The pain was evident in her voice.

Abigail was sure there had to be more to the story.

Her theory was only confirmed when he said, "I am truly sorry." in the most sincere voice.

But she couldn't uncover it now. He was going to die. Both of the men that she and Daphne loved were either going to die or be ridden from society. The weight of what was happening kept growing in the form of a pit at the bottom of her stomach.

"We need to go, Daph, before anyone should see us." She heard Anthony say from far off.

He took his sister, and began to walk out of the maze before he stopped.

"Abby?" He turned and questioned, as if expecting her to follow.

"Don't." she said and headed off in the opposite direction. They couldn't have gone in together anyway.

As she walked, she could hear her thoughts screaming inside her head.

He's going to die. He's going to die or he's going to leave. Is there nothing you can do?

Chapter 18

Abigail tiptoed across the hard wood floors on the hallway of the Bridgerton household. She had informed her maid and the household staff that she would be staying there for the night, making some excuse about Daphne and herself not wanting to separate. In reality, she simply couldn't leave when she knew Anthony was about to ride off to either his death or his exile. Her maid had dressed her for bed and tied her hair in a plat, but she knew she couldn't sit and do nothing. So, she slipped on her flats and now was making her way to Daphne's room.

Knocking softly, she didn't wait for a response before slipping into the room. As it would appear, Daphne was up and pacing.

"I see you couldn't sleep either." Abigail said.

"How could I?" Daphne threw her arms up exasperatedly. "Either way, I have a man I love's death on my hands!" She shouted in a whisper.

"Well then, what are we going to do?" Abby questioned, needing a solution.

"What can we do?" Daphne echoed, continuing to pace. "They are completely stubborn, and idiotic and they have no reason to—" but she stopped mid sentence.

"Daph?" Abby prompted, stepping closer.

"We were seen." Daphne whispered in shock.

"What?"

"Cressida Cowper." Daphne whipped around to face her. "She-she asked me if I caught a chill in the garden... oh my god." Her hand flew to her mouth.

After a few moments of pure shock, Abigail sprung into action.

"Right. Here's what we're to do."

—-

Anthony gave Simon a hard, loathing stare as their seconds inspected the guns. He hated him. Hated him for defiling his sister. Hated him for ripping himself of any chance of happiness within society. He didn't even get to say goodbye to Abigail. Not that he didn't try, but she wouldn't acknowledge him after they arrived home. He didn't care though. It was easier, if they made a clean break now.

"For what it is worth," Simon's voice pulled him from his thoughts. "I am sorry."

"Your apology is worth nothing to me." He spit back almost immediately.

His brother handed him his gun and both men turned back to back, cocking their pistols.

"Ready!" He called.

"Ready." He heard in response from behind him.

They each began to take, slow, methodical steps forward.

One. Two. Three... he counted in his head. Purposefully, he shoved all other thoughts aside.

Ten.

He began to turn and as he did so, watched as Simon stuck his pistol to the sky. He stretched his own out, pausing for a moment as determination set in his eyes. Then he fired.

Only after the bullet had left the gun did he hear the voice of his sister yell, "Stop!"

She fell from her horse, landing motionless on the ground.

"Daphne!"

"Sister!"

They both ran toward her as she lay, sprawled on the ground. Landing on the grass in front of her, he felt the panic rise, then immediately drop, as she began to move.

"Oh, good God." He let out.

"Are you hurt? Tell me!" The Duke insisted, not moving from the spot in front of her.

She began to stand and said, "I am perfectly well, no thanks to you idiots."

"What the hell do you think you're playing at?" Anthony questioned in aggravation.

"Says the man who just shot at me!" She replied with a comeback.

"You just rode into the middle of a duel!" He continued to shout.

She took a breath before saying, "I require a moment with the Duke."

"Daphne—"Anthony tried to interrupt but Daphne insisted.

"I require a moment with the Duke." She said with finality.

Benedict separated them and Anthony watched as they both walked off to have a private conversation. What they were saying he did not know, but he looked around to see who had brought her here, and noticed Colin. After giving him a rather pointed look, he scanned further, but did not see anyone else who was not already there.

He wasn't sure what he was hoping for. Maybe just to see her. But he assured himself that this was the last place he would want to find her.

Having had enough he walked forward and interrupt-ed.

"We must resume before someone should find us." He stated.

The Duke walked back toward them but before they could even get a hand on their pistols Daphne's voice rang out.

"There will be no need to resume. The Duke and I are to be married." She announced.

Everyone stared at her in shock. Several moments passed before he finally came to his senses. He was about to protest but before he could, he heard a horse let out a cry to his left. Turning, he saw Abigail, wearing a cloak similar to Daphne's to cover her night dress, and her hair blowing out of its plat as she rode the horse with great speed. It grew closer and came to a swift halt. She only said a few words.

"The police will be here in five minutes. I haven't given them any names, just a location." She locked eyes with him. "I suggest you scatter."

And with that she motioned to Daphne, who got back on her own horse and they rode off in the same direc-tion, leaving all the men momentarily in shock as they stared after them.

Chapter 19

♥

"How does it feel Sister, to be in love?" Hyacinth asked as she bounced down the stairs with the rest of the Bridgerton women, Abigail included.

"Imagine leaping off the cliff and shattering on the ground. A fair analogy?" Eloise responded for Daphne.

"I am afraid I cannot find the words dear Hyacinth." Daphne said with an air of inattention in her voice. "Though, Eloise, I do believe you will know what love feels like soon enough next season."

"You think I am to follow in your footsteps, Sister? Could there be a more dreadful fate?" Eloise clapped back.

"El." Abigail warned as the younger Bridgerton passed by her.

"You do know that I am setting the standard or your future matches, Yes? You should be grateful." Daphne snapped with some misdirected anger.

"The only thing I am grateful for is that I am not you, nor will I ever be." Eloise responded with just as much resentment in her tone.

"Alright, you two. Take a step back-- please." Abigail encouraged, and with that Eloise walked away.

"I should be off." Abby announced gathering the gloves that were laid out for her on the table as well as her coin purse. "Thank you for allowing me to stay the night, Violet." She thanked the woman with a small curtsy and wiggled her gloves on.

"Oh, darling, if you are free after tea time we'd love to see you at the Modiste. Daphne has to be fitted for her trousseau, and I'd love to order you another gown while we are there."

"Oh... Lady Bridgerton, that's very kind, but not necessary." She attempted to decline.

"For the thousandth time it's Violet, and I don't want to hear a word about that. I am buying you another gown and that's final." She said with an air of motherly command about her voice.

Abigail smiled to herself as a maid helped her into her tailored coat.

"Yes ma'am." She said softly, still reveling in the warm, safe feeling those words just brought her.

"Abby!" Daphne said as Abigail was trying to turn around.

She ran over to her friend and gave her a tight hug.

She whispered in her ear, "Thank you for everything this morning."

She then pulled back and squeezed her hand before being called away by a footman announcing a visit from the Prince. Leaving before she could become involved with that, Abigail finally turned around and made her way to the doorway.

Before she could get there, however, the doors opened and Anthony stepped through. He tried to catch her eye but she simply ducked her head down and refused to meet his gaze as she passed him out the doorway. His body turned to watch her go, and he felt a sense of longing. He knew something had changed between them, but he couldn't know the problem if she refused to even look at him.

"Your wedding gown is a long way from being finished Miss Bridgerton. I promise you will not be disappointed." Madame Delacroix assured her as she pinned the bottom of Daphne's Wedding dress.

Abigail smiled as she watched from her spot next to the fabrics on display. Daphne already looked stunning in the basic format of the gown. The final product would be a sight to see. "She will need a new pelisse too, and then the more intimate items." Violet added instructions to the modiste. "Four nightdresses, perhaps? Or five?"

"What could I possibly need with five new nightdresses?" Daphne scoffed from her place in front of the mirror.

This made Abigail pause. She did know what happened on a wedding night... didn't she?

"They are not for you, ma chère, but for your amoureux." Madame Delacroix. "What else do you think a honeymoon is for?"

Did she know what a honeymoon was for? Abigail was now growing increasingly concerned.

"It will be a most special time, dear." Her mother assured her.

That was the icing on the cake, Daphne definitely had no idea what she was walking into.

"Yes, five. Five nightdresses will do nicely." Violet chuckled as she gave the final instructions.

Madame Delacroix got up and signaled she would be back in a moment when Abby heard the shop door open and close behind her. She was going to turn to see who had arrived, but in mere moments Cressida Cowper was striding passed her to approach Daphne. She was practically crooning.

"Daphne, how lovely to see you. Oh, I do hope your wedding dress will be ready in time. Madame Delacroix must be working fast." She greeted with a sickly sweet voice.

Abigail knew it wasn't proper for a young lady to feel pure hate or spite towards a person, but sometimes it seemed as if the universe liked to test her patience.

"Mama, might you spare me a moment? I must have Cressida's opinion on some fabric. Her taste is impeccable." Daphne fibbed.

"Of course, dear." Her mother responded.

Daphne walked Cressida over to where Abigail stood, next to the rolls of displayed fabric.

"I am to have a new pelisse for my honeymoon. What about this color? Trimmed with fur, perhaps."

Abigail wondered how long they would dance around the obvious before someone brought up last night's events.

"Fur at this time of year?" Cressida questioned. "Well, I suppose it depends on how much time you and the Duke spend outdoors. But you are fond of a midnight garden stroll, I believe."

And there it was.

"I do not know what you mean." Daphne said, attempting to keep a light air about their conversation.

"I am almost certain I saw the two of you in the gardens at the Trowbridge ball. No chaperone in sight." She vaguely threatened.

"How strange." Daphne responded. "I do not recall leaving the ballroom. Though I dare say it would have been difficult to see the gardens with any real clarity at night, unless you were actually out in them yourself."

"My view of the garden was perfectly clear from the safety of the terrace, Daphne." Cressida defended quickly, then swooped like a bird of prey. "You dallied with the Prince purely to rouse the Duke's jealousy, then you lured him into those gardens to trap him into marriage. I never would have imagined that a Bridgerton would ever come to know such shame."

Fed up with her demeanor, Abigail cut in.

"You should consider your words more carefully, Cressida. In a matter of days, Daphne is to be a Duchess, and you are to be just as you are now, unmarried and untitled. So you can either be a Duchess's friend or her enemy. I have chosen friend, but it is entirely up to you." She practically spit the words at her.

"Oh, you are one to talk, Abigail. I know you were with the Viscount Bridgerton that same night, in those same gardens. I only spared mentioning it because you weren't my enemy, don't make me change my mind."

At her words Daphne look towards Abigail with shock and hurt written on her face. She hadn't told her. She should have, but she had so much going on. The last thing Abigail needed to do was burden her with the complications involving her brother.

"As for you Daphne," Cressida continued. "I'd like to first see if you drag him down the aisle at all. I would imagine a man like the Duke, does not take kindly to being forced into anything."

With her final scathing words she left the two young women staring blankly in front of them, utterly scared and unsure of what to do.

Chapter 20

Anthony stood in the midst of the pews as he heard the church bells ringing in the distance. He contemplated his surroundings and recalled a time when he used to run from the prospect of having to walk down this aisle one day. Now, it felt different. Now, when he thought of walking down the aisle for her, all feelings of dread he might have had melted away.

But he shook himself free of these thoughts. That was not why he was here. He was here for his sister, not Abigail. No matter how much he wished it were different.

Did she still want to marry him? She hadn't even spoken to him in the past day. What was going on?

"Apologies for my tardiness" The Duke's voice echoed as he entered the chapel.

"Not at all." Anthony assured. "The archbishop is yet to arrive."

The two men stood next to each other in the middle of the aisle, an awkward silence passing between them. No doubt, both were recalling the last time they were together, in which each had a gun pointed at the other.

It took several more awkward moments to pass before Anthony finally broke the silence.

"We should discuss the matter of Daphne's dowry." He began, but the Duke responded with the speed of light.

"There is nothing to discuss. I will not accept one."

Caught off guard, Anthony said, "I beg your pardon?"

"I need not be paid to marry Daphne. It is frankly an insulting custom in my judgement. You may place the money in trust for her, if you'd like." Simon further explained. "But you need not harbor any doubts of my intentions to support your sister. Her well being is my responsibility now. I take that duty with the utmost seriousness."

This was not something Anthony was expecting. Far from being angry with him anymore, he was impressed. Realizing Simon most likely deserved an apology, he shifted the conversation.\

"I must apologize for, uh... well..." He could not seem to find a polite or delicate way to state his words.

"Shooting at me?" Simon supplied in a much more blunt manor.

"Indeed." Anthony confirmed.

Simon chuckled softly at this.

"I would have thought you dishonorable had you not." Simon assured. "Besides you have always been a terrible shot. I mean surely, you'd have stood a greater chance of wounding me if you had simply fired straight up in the air." He joked.

Anthony, who assumed he should have been offended, simply laughed. Glad they were able to joke again.

"May I speak freely?" The Duke asked.

"I dare say you've earned it." Anthony responded.

"Are you..." He paused. "What is Miss Bentley to you now?" Simon finally asked. "The last I checked things were 'complicated', as you so wittingly put it, and now I know something must have happened for she was with you in the garden as well."

"Ah, yes... I suppose you must think me a hypocrite to have been alone with a lady as well." Guessed Anthony.

"I don't know what to think, that is why I am asking." Simon assured.

"I asked her to marry me." He said simply.

The Duke gave a boisterous laugh and clapped him on the shoulder.

"Well done, Bridgerton!" But then he paused and his grip loosened. "She did say yes didn't she?"

"Yes. Yes she did. And for a half a second, we were happy. But um, something's changed. Since the duel she hasn't looked at me or spoken to me... I just wish she would tell me what is going on." He trailed off, more thinking aloud.

Simon squeezed his shoulder once more before letting his hand drop and saying, "Why is it you can never do anything simply."

Anthony scoffed.

"Oh you're one to talk!"

He laughed and said, "Yes I suppose I am."

Which caused them both to laugh and not notice the archbishop's arrival until he was nearly standing next to them.

"Oh, Your Grace." Anthony greeted and walked forward. "May I express my gratitude for your granting of this special license."

"Perhaps, my lord, you should not." The archbishop announced.

Simon and Anthony furrowed their brows and turned to look at each other. This was not going to be good.

"Did you think I wouldn't want to know?" Daphne paced back in the Bridgerton foyer.

Both she and Abigail had arrived home from the modiste and Daphne, to put it plainly, was livid with Abigail for not informing her about her involvement with her brother.

"Well, in all fairness you did know... sort of." Abigail defended from her stationary position as she watched Daphne continue to pace.

"I knew you were flirting. I knew you were taken with each other. What I did not know was that he had proposed, or that he had also taken you out into that garden."

"Daphne, you were upset and hurt over the Duke. The last thing I wanted to do was throw my happy relationship in your face." Abby continued to plead her case.

"Well, you do not get to decide what information I should and should not have!" Daphne cut her off with a harsh tone.

"Hey!" Abigail wasn't having any more of this. "I admit that I should have told you, but at the moment, I think you are misdirecting some anger, and I'd like it not to be directed towards me!"

She'd never had a fight with a friend before. Young ladies aren't taught to handle conflict. But she and Daphne were close and despite how horrid the conversation was going, she knew it was only because they cared about each other.

"Sorry to interrupt." Anthony's voice said as he and the Duke entered the foyer.

Both she and Daphne, annoyed with the interruption, rolled their eyes and backed away from each other.

Abigail placed a hand on the bridge of her nose as Daphne said, "Well? How did it go with the archbishop?"

"Not well in fact." Anthony announced. "We were, well, denied our request for a special license."

This caught their attention. Both of them froze in shock. Abigail's gears began turning. What possible reason could the archbishop have to deny the license?

"Denied?" Daphne repeated. "What on earth for?"

"For some reason the Archbishop of Canterbury did not think he owed me an explanation." He explained.

This meant he didn't have an explanation. So who was really pulling the strings?

"If we are to wait weeks for this wedding, it gives Cressida Cowper, who had much to say about you two by the way..." Daphne gestured between Abigail and Anthony.

Anthony looked up at her, his eyes wide. Finally, Abigail looked him in the eyes, and slowly nodded. He took a deep breath. This just became much more complicated. Daphne's voice pulled them back to reality.

"... not to mention Whistledown, and anyone else, far too much time to uncover the truth of what happened in that garden."

Her words hung in the air. Both couples either staring at each other or staring at the ground. Abigail was one of the latter, partially because she was still working out why the license would be denied, and partially so she didn't have to meet Anthony's gaze.

"Lady Danbury." A footman announced and the intimidating woman entered the room.

"Welcome!" Violet said as she also entered the foyer. "Welcome! Is everyone as famished as I?" She chuckled.

A few moments of silence passed between the room as each young person exchanged glances.

"Now, this is far too grim a mood for the celebration I was counting on. What on earth is the matter?" Lady Danbury questioned.

"Anthony?" Lady Bridgerton prompted.

"We have been denied our request for a special license." Anthony explained.

"What?"

"The archbishop did not see a need." Simon added.

That is when it clicked in Abigail's head.

She gasped lightly and said, "It's not the archbishop. It's the Queen."

"Precisely what I was to say, my dear." Lady Danbury validated. "Perhaps she has taken Miss Bridgerton's rejection of her nephew to heart, or perhaps she is simply bored." She turned to look at Violet. "Either way, it does not bode well for your daughter's social future, nor any of the Bridgertons for that matter."

"Surely we must be able to do something." Said Violet.

Lady Danbury paused for a moment before saying, "Give her what she wants. Attention. Appear before her yourselves and make a personal appeal. But she will not respond to begging and she can sniff out even the faintest whiff of insincerity, so do not lay it on thick... tell her you are in love. Plain, and simple, and true." She looked between the two before asking, "You can do that, can you not?"

The two looked at each other before each nodding their heads in affirmation.

"Good. Now, where is the dinner I was promised?" She returned to her cheery mood and followed Violet to the dining room.

They each followed, first Simon, then Daphne after him. Then, Abigail walked past Anthony as his eyes followed her. Soon enough, he followed her inside and thought to himself how he'd like to talk to her alone. He just wasn't sure how to make that happen.

Chapter 21

Abigail sat in a row to herself as the Bridgerton family around her conversed with either each other, or the guests on Simon's side of the church. Violet turned from the row in front of her and reached for her hand.

Giving it a light squeeze she said, "Just think dear, it might be you walking down this aisle next."

Abigail smiled and squeezed back, while trying to ignore the squirm in her stomach, or the flutter in her heart when she thought of the man who had proposed mere days before.

"Someday." she replied. "But today, I'm beyond happy for Daphne."

It looked as if Violet would have said something else, but the string quartet began to play, signaling Daphne's arrival. Every member in the pews stood and turned to see her walking down the aisle beside her brother.

She looked angelic, and Abigail watched as Daphne grew nearer the Duke and their eyes didn't separate from each other. That must be nice, to have someone with whom to share a connection, a bond.

Once she reached the altar, Anthony smiled and let her go. The next thing Abigail knew, Anthony was sitting next to her.

"Dearly beloved..." the bishop started.

Abigail tried to ignore his presence. She was mad at him, and she wouldn't be swayed by his proximity, or his irritatingly intoxicating scent.

"We are gathered here today..."

All strength left her body when she felt a hand, his hand, reach for hers. Their fingers interlocked and she took a deep breath. This wasn't good. His mere touch made her want to throw out all feelings of anger. Something told her he knew this.

"It is said that marriage hath in it less of beauty, but more of safety than the single life."

She spared a glance toward him. Her eyes flitted rightward and she knew he noticed. He smiled slightly and gave her hand a squeeze, causing another flutter to happen in her heart.

"I now pronounce you man and wife."

With these words, her fingers relaxed within his grip. There was something strangely comforting about those words. Those words, and his presence. The combination felt so... safe.

"So happy for you. Thank you for inviting us." Abigail heard as she approached Daphne with a glass of water.

Those who were congratulating her left, and Abby sidled next to her.

"Here." She said, and held out the glass.

"What, no wine left?" Daphne questioned.

She took the glass and basically downed the liquid in one gulp.

"Daph, the last thing you need right now is alcohol." Abigail countered.

"Fair enough." Daphne said nervously, and glanced over to where the Duke was.

"Have you talked to him yet?" Abby asked.

"No." She sighed. "Have you talked to my brother yet?"

"No." Abby replied.

"Abigail—" Daphne began.

"No." She cut off. "The minute we start talking, it will turn into a large screaming match, and I just cannot do that right now. And certainly not here."

"Again, fair enough." Daphne said. "Do you—"

But she didn't get to finish her thought as Cressida had approached the two.

"I suppose congratulations are in order." Her voice was sickly sweet. "We being friends, after all." This made

Abigails eyes roll, which did not go unnoticed. "I do hope you will remember my kindness in keeping secrets, and repay me someday. Let us hope Abigail can be as triumphant as you." Her tone had shifted into something more threatening, then she walked off.

"On second thought," Abigail began, her breathing became quick. "Alcohol seems like a wonderful idea."

Separating herself from Daphne, she picked up her skirt slightly, and worked her way through the crowd. When almost to the table filled with drinks and cakes, she felt a hand on her wrist and her body was now being pulled. Slipping through people as if they were vapors, it took her a moment to realize she was being pulled by none other than Anthony Bridgerton. He finally stopped when they had reached the edge of the foyer.

Turning on the spot, he didn't waste time.

"I don't like this. Why won't you talk to me?" He stated, bluntly.

Abigail looked about the room, and aside from a glance or two from a Bridgerton sibling, everyone else seemed to be too wrapped up in their own conversations to notice them.

"Is this honestly the time or the place?" She tried to skip around the accusation.

"Well I'd love to talk about this somewhere else, but you are so skilled at avoiding me that I do not see much of another option." He replied as if he'd been expecting her response.

"Well what can I say, I have a gift." She switched to sarcasm.

He groaned.

"Abigail, talk to me please. We are engaged, do you even still want to marry me?"

"Do I—" she stopped and swiftly looked around the room, acutely aware that Whistledown could physically be in their presence.

Taking a deep breath she said, "Of course I still want to marry you."

"Alright then—"

"But I cannot pretend that you didn't just voluntarily give up our life together when you challenged that duel." Her voice was on the verge of cracking.

"It was a case of my family's honor—"

She put a hand on his chest to cut him off, then swiftly removed it, still being aware of the very public nature of this conversation.

"And I understand that, more than anyone. But I cannot live knowing my life could shift due some spur of the moment decision you make." She was practically forcing out the words now.

"Abigail..." His voice softened.

"You should check in with your sister. I'm sure the party doesn't have much longer to go." She simply said and walked off before she would cry.

Taking very long, very deep breaths, she searched for the refreshment table. Finding it, she reached for the bowl filled with lemonade and ladled some into a crystal glass. She drank two entire glasses before she felt as if she wouldn't let any tears slip. Gathering a third, she stepped back towards the wall and slowly sipped it, lost in her own thoughts.

"You are going to have to forgive him at some point you know." She heard from next to her.

While normally she would expect a Bridgerton sibling, this time she was surprised to see the Duke standing next to her.

Looking up at him, she replied.

"What are you? His wingman? Spare me."

"You have an interest in my best friend, Miss Bentley."

He was going to say more but she spoke before he could do so.

"And you just married mine, Your Grace." She quirked her eyebrow.

It took a moment but eventually, he laughed. It was somewhat infectious, and soon enough she was laughing too.

"Touché." He finally chuckled. "But I say this with complete seriousness. I've never seen him so taken with one woman before. And I've known him a very long time."

She blushed, but looked down to pretend she didn't.

"Besides," He carried on. "I may need some support if I'm to be the only in-law of this family."

She laughed and was thankful for the uptick in her mood.

"Your Grace," a footman approached them. "We are bringing the carriages around."

"Right, thank you." Simon said, and was about to leave before Abigail's gloved hand caught his arm.

"My turn to be serious. I, if anyone, know how complicated yours and Daphne's courtship was. Promise me you will actually talk to each other now."

He smiled and said, "I promise."

"Good." She said and began to walk alongside him out the door. "Because I really don't think I could take a letter a day from Daphne. I mean, I'm happy for you two, but your relationship should stay your own." She cracked another joke.

They both laughed and talked until the rest of the Bridgertons came swarming out the house, Daphne in the lead. After a tearful goodbye and many hugs from each family member, Abigail included, Daphne finally stepped into the carriage and the Duke followed her.

As they rode off and she waved, Abigail became now increasingly aware that she could no longer hide behind anything. With Daphne's wedding over, she would have to either work everything out with Anthony, or call off the engagement. Neither sounded like a very enjoyable option.

Chapter 22

Eloise was reading the Whistledown sheet aloud as they all sat in the guest room, which as Hyacinth had pointed out, was basically Abby's now.

Abigail was finishing getting ready and Violet was with her. Abby was sure she was missing Daphne and was wanting to pour her energy into something else, so she was happy to be that distraction for her.

"What did she mean by stamina when she was congratulating Daphne?" Eloise wondered aloud.

Abby looked up and caught Violet's eye in the mirror as she put her earring in. They both widened their eyes slightly and Abigail quickly made an excuse.

"I'm sure it was just yet another adjective the woman decided to throw in."

"You know, I was thinking." Hyacinth started.

"Well that's a shock." Eloise said with a drawl to her tone.

"Eloise!" Violet scolded. "Thinking about what, dear?"

"I was only going to say," She threw a pointed look at her sister. "That Abigail's practically our sister now."

Abby immediately froze. Not because she was offended, but because she knew how much she wanted to be, and how close she almost was to actually being their sister.

"Well that's very sweet of you to say dear." Violet said and moved forward to place a hand on Abigail's shoulder. "Now I don't want you putting any kind of pressure on yourself today, alright?" Her thumb rubbed comforting circles. "Just because Daphne is gone does not mean I have stopped thinking of your match. We will simply give this the proper time it needs."

Abby smiled in the mirror and simply nodded, not knowing what she could say in response that would communicate how very loved she felt at that moment.

"Alright now, everybody out! We need to get going." She announced to her two daughters, and Eloise groaned to leave the room while Hyacinth practically skipped off. "Meet us downstairs, dear." She said before exiting the room.

Abby nodded and turned to grab her shawl, but before she could, she noticed movement outside her door. And in almost seconds, Anthony was in her room and had lightly shut the door behind him.

"Anthony what are you—" but she didn't get to finish.

"Shh! I just— I had to talk to you before we left." He said.

So she stood there and waited for him to say something. He took a deep breath before finally voicing his thoughts.

"I just want you to know that when I was out in that field with Hastings, all I could think about was you."

Abigail sucked in a breath. She wasn't expecting that.

"I make impulsive decisions. I do before I think. And I know it's wrong, but I honestly don't see that changing." He took another breath as if what he was going to say next was hard. "If that is something you can't live with... I understand. But I just— I needed you to know."

He moved to leave but her arm reached out and caught him before he could. He turned to look at her and he saw the troubled look on her face. There were tears welling in her eyes but he couldn't tell why.

"...There are worse things to live with." She said, finally.

He paused. He wasn't hearing this right.

"I won't believe it until you say the words." He said.

With a small chuckle she moved her eyes from the carpet and looked into his brown ones.

"Anthony Bridgeton, if you would still have me, I would love to marry you."

She had barely finished the sentence before his lips were on hers. She could feel his smile and immediately mimicked it. He picked her up and spun her as if he was the happiest man on earth. He certainly felt like it at the moment.

"Please tell me we can announce this." He pulled away and asked with a sense of childlike excitement in his voice.

She laughed, and nodded vigorously. He kissed her again.

"Thank God. We'll do it at the garden party today, I'm not waiting another second." He announced.

With another quick kiss, and much more joyful laughing on her part, he hurried out of the room.

The crowd chattered and Abigail stood with Violet and Eloise, sipping her champagne. As she observed the lovely scenery, she couldn't remember ever feeling this happy.

"I wonder what Daphne's doing at this very moment." Hyacinth wondered from Violet's side.

Abigail held back a snort as she was sure she knew exactly what she and Simon were doing.

"I am sure she has many new duties to attend to as Duchess. There are things you should be learning yourself to prepare for your debut." She nudged Eloise, who scoffed.

"Making simpering conversation, pretending not to wince every time a man treads on my toes during a waltz?" Eloise responded sarcastically.

"Eloise!" Violet tried to scold but was distracted as Gregory pulled Hyacinth away and they ran off.

"I'm no good at those things mama. I shall only make a fool of myself." Eloise carried on.

"Well perhaps if you devoted as much time to your deportment lessons as you did to writing in your journal, you might feel rather better."

Abigail sipped her champagne and noted how they really could go round and round with each other. She moved away from them and casually joined the conversation with Anthony and Benedict.

Anthony's smile widened and she practically lit up being nearer to him.

"You ready?" He asked.

She was about to respond with a very happy 'yes', but before she could do so she heard a glass clinking not four feet from them. Turning, she saw Colin who was gaining everyone's attention.

"Pray, may I have everyone's attention?" He began. "I would like to make a small but rather important announcement. I have happy news to impart. I have asked Miss Marina Thompson to be my wife, and she has accepted."

While everyone around her began smiling and cheering, even some applauding, Abigail felt as if the world had gone quiet. With the pit in her stomach she looked to her left to see Anthony, with a very similar expression on his face.

She reached over in a small movement and grasped his hand tightly. They would be able to be together someday. At least she hoped.

Chapter 23

"You barely know the young lady, what were you thinking?" Anthony was livid.

He had just pushed Colin into his study, who, much to his annoyance, seemed all too calm with his brother's anger.

"I was thinking you'd respond like this and how little I would care to hear it." Colin responded, and sat nicely on one of the many armchairs.

"Do you think this is a joke?" Anthony almost laughed at his ignorance. "Poor Mother was beside herself."

"Mother seems perfectly happy to me. She congratulated us." Colin defended.

Anthony paused and backed up, he couldn't think of another reason he would marry this girl he barely knew.

"So, you compromised this young lady?" He accused.

"Certainly not. I am a gentleman."

"Then why ever would you—"

"Why does anyone marry, brother? For love, of course."

Anthony couldn't stop himself before he laughed, scoffed, even.

"Love? Oh dear God, what do you know of love?"

"Oh and you know something about it?" Colin stood, offended.

"I certainly know more than you!" They were practically shouting at each other now.

"Oh and which young lady has had the fortune of your proposal?" Colin asked, incredulously.

"That'd be me." Abigail said from the doorway, a voice of calm in the storm.

In all the shouting, neither two men noticed how she had opened the door and was leaning against the archway.

"Wha--" Colin looked between the two. "You two?"

They looked at each other with a sort of longing. Colin was overtook with a wave of guilt, not so much towards his brother, for he was much too stubborn and had insulted Marina, but towards Abigail.

"Oh, Abigail I'm— I'm so sorry." Colin walked toward her in an attempt to show his sincerity.

"It's alright Colin." Abby responded with politeness in her tone.

Anthony scoffed, it was very much not alright from his perspective. Abigail gave him a look, then turned her attention back towards his brother.

"I am happy for you. We'll figure something out."

Colin smiled and for the first time recognized how wonderful of a person she was. He didn't know what she saw in his brother. He cleared his throat and turned back to Anthony.

"If I caused mother discomfort today then I am sorry for it. I shall speak with her." His words were now formal. "And I am now aware that I have stood in your way, and I do apologize for that... but I would still very much prefer your blessing."

"Then I am afraid I must disappoint you." Anthony responded from his chair.

"You have... in more ways than one." With that, Colin walked past Abigail and exited the study at a brisk pace.

Abigail stayed in her place, with her arms crossed and her body facing towards the bookshelves.

"You're too harsh with him." She noted while looking at the floor, apparently thinking.

"Oh, not you too." Anthony stood and made a beeline for his drink cart.

"Ever think that if something is repeated to you, it might be for a reason?" She watched his back as he poured the brown liquid into a crystal glass.

Once the glass was in hand, he turned and locked eyes with her, his eyes clearly still ablaze with anger.

"Abigail— not only did he wreck every hope of announcing our engagement, but he has made our lives ten times more complicated in the process, and my mother—"

"Hey." She cut him off by putting her hands on either side of his face.

He took a deep breath and closed his eyes, enjoying her calming presence and her intoxicating scent.

"We are going to figure this out." She assured him in what she hoped was a firm voice.

He set his drink down and brought his hands up to hers, moving her palm so he could kiss it. It was these moments that made her sure that this was going to work.

"Do you never doubt?" He asked in a soft voice.

He needed reassurance. He was vulnerable right now.

"It took me a moment to realize, but now I know. For as much trouble as this relationship may bring, it's worth it."

She leaned upward to kiss his cheek. However, she was intercepted as his face turned and he caught her on the lips. She smiled, as did he, and they both felt an immense happiness at that moment.

"Alright," She pulled back. "Here's what we're to do."

He nodded his head in acknowledgment, and his hands snaked around her back, while hers found his shirt collar.

"You are going to gage your mother's reaction to Colin's announcement, and see how soon we can talk to her. I am going to go home and talk to my father." She announced the last part rather begrudgingly.

Anthony immediately began shaking his head.

"No. I don't like you going over there. The whole point of you having a room here was so you wouldn't have to go back home as often."

"Anthony, he would never hurt me... physically."

"If you are going then I am coming with you." He tried to insist.

"No." She said.

"Abigail—"

"No. My father and I have some words that need to be said, and you really do not need to see that."

He sighed, frustrated. "Alright. But you come back afterwards."

"Aye aye, Captain." She chuckled.

"You make light, but I'm serious." He squeezed her waist to further make his point.

"I understand." She assured.

Leaning up to give him a quick kiss, she pulled away. Before turning around, she spotted his half filled drink on his desk. Without thinking, she reached for it and threw it back, feeling the need for a little liquid courage. Handing him the glass as he wore an impressed look upon his face, she turned and exited his study with determination.

Chapter 24

With a deep breath, Abigail twisted the doorknob to her father's study. Upon entering she was met immediately with the overwhelming scent of alcohol and tobacco.

"Oh good Lord." She muttered as she navigated her way through the piles of newspaper and debris.

"Hm? Who's there?" Said the lump in the armchair.

"Your daughter?" She responded sarcastically.

She didn't like who she became around him. Resentful, sarcastic, and most of all, guarded. It wasn't an immediate instinct. She had to learn how to handle conversing with him after her mother died.

He wasn't the same either, to be fair. Gone was the man who danced her around the parlor or brought candy floss home to her. Her father wasn't there anymore. Now, all that sat before her was a broken shell of a man she had once known.

"No, my daughter isn't home right now." He shook his head and slumped further into his chair.

"I can assure you she is. Since she is me." She replied, moving some stacks of newspapers.

"I like that riddle." He laughed and brought his glass to his lips, to which Abby rolled her eyes.

"Father, as hard as it is, I need you to pay attention right now." She attempted to speak but he just acted as if no one was there.

She sighed and knew there was likely only one thing that was going to get him to acknowledge her.

"I'm getting married." She announced.

He froze. His lazy and relaxed demeanor was gone, and replaced with one of a deer on the wrong end of a rifle.

"What?" He grunted.

"Anthony Bridgerton has asked for my hand and I have accepted."

"No." He began to get up, though very sloppily. "No. Your suitors are supposed to come talk to me. I- I make this decision."

"You lost every right you had to make that decision when you left me alone in this situation. When you left me to parent the boys." She responded with the speed of light.

"I didn't leave. I'm right here, Abby." He tried to appeal.

She took a deep breath so as to keep her emotions in check.

"At some point after mother died, you made the decision to drown your sorrows in bourbon rather than be a father."

"That is not true!" He became angry and defensive. "Losing your mother was the hardest thing that has ever happened to me! You don't understand—"

"Oh I don't? It was hard for all of us! I lost my mother the very moment I needed her most! But you know what I did? I got over it, because I had a job to do and because the boys needed me!" She lost it-- all control over her emotions.

The anger, the grief, the tears, it all came tumbling out. It was almost as if she had held it in for so long that she couldn't contain it anymore.

"You wasted away all the time you had to step up! So I did what I had to, I took control." She took a slow and controlled breath. "I am marrying Anthony Bridgerton and I am going to be very happy, very far from you. I think it'd be best if you retired to the country house, that way I can say that you're ill and have gone away at the wedding."

"You cannot just—"

"I can just. While I wish that some part of you would put down the bottle and pick up the last shred of self respect you have left, I know you won't. So, I need you gone so that I can keep this house and the Bentley name in order for Ben and Cal when they grow up." She said far too calmly. "I will arrange your travel plans with Mrs. Whiler, she will give you all the information you need."

She then turned and moved to exit the study.

"Abigail." She heard him say quietly.

She paused with her hand near the doorknob and twisted her head to look behind her.

"Yes?" She kept her tone formal.

"I wish things could have been different." He said after a few moments.

The last nail in the coffin. Things could never change, he would never let them.

"Me too. You have no idea how much."

With those final words, she twisted the doorknob and left the study.

Chapter 25

Dear Abigail,

I'm afraid this letter is much overdue, but I have been rather preoccupied since I arrived at Clyvedon. Before you laugh whilst reading this, I did not mean anything improper. Although, admittedly, such improper things did happen quite often.

I am not sure if you know or do not know what I am talking about, but I feel the need to tell you, that marriage is not what we were fooled into thinking it was.

I do not wish to trouble you, but married life has proven more difficult than I had imagined. I believed that whatever troubles came our way, Simon and I would face them together, but I have since learned he has been keeping secrets from me.

He has made a horrendous vow to his late father that the Hastings line will die with him. Again, I do not wish to be graphic but his inability to have children is not so much an inability, as a grudge he chooses to keep.

I am writing this letter because I require council, and Lord knows I cannot ask Mama. She sent me into the lion's den unprepared, I highly doubt she will understand the gravity of this situation. I need your help Abby. I miss my best friend. Write to me.

With all my love,

Daphne

Bridgerton,

How are you? I hope things with Miss Bentley have worked themselves out since we left you. I do not know if you have announced anything yet, or even told your family but I wish you luck.

Well, I wish you luck and I caution you. I do not mean to sound melancholy, but marriage is proving more of a feat than I had anticipated. I certainly do not wish to overshare nor burden you with the troubles of my life nor your sister's, but I implore you to think carefully about the decision you and Miss Bentley are about to make.

Once married, nothing is your own anymore. Not your thoughts nor your decisions. I would never tell you not to do something that would make you happy, but please, think about it clearly beforehand.

That is really all I had wished to say.

Sincerely,

Hastings

Chapter 26

Abigail made her way down the street with Daphne's letter in hand. It was early in the morning and it had been an uneasy two days since the confrontation with her father. She had stayed at the house partly because she was too emotionally exhausted to leave, but also because she had to now get the family affairs in order if her father was to move to the country home.

She spent all of yesterday in the study attempting to make sense of the millions of papers that related to her family's affairs, all the while the staff were packing her father's things for him to move.

The letter from Daphne had arrived in the early morning post, and she made her way back to the Bridgerton household. She had decided to walk instead of take a carriage, the contents of the letter whirling in her mind.

"..Marriage is not what we were fooled into thinking it was."

"...Have since learned he has been keeping secrets from me."

For some reason, Abigail was not surprised. Of course, with everything that had happened during their courtship something like this would arise. She felt for Daphne, but what could she tell her? It's not as if she had been married herself nor had any perspective. No, it seemed as if the universe were providing one obstacle after another in order to prevent her from marrying.

Lost in thought, she hardly noticed the boy running down the streets holding the latest copies of Whistle-down. Well, that was she hardly noticed until he was right next to her.

"Oh wait a moment!" She called, effectively stopping him.

Pulling some money from the coin purse around her wrist, she handed it to the boy and he gave her a fresh sheet before running off.

All is fair in love and war, but some battles leave no victor, only a trail of broken hearts that makes us won-der if the price we pay is ever worth the fight. The ones we love have the power to inflict the greatest scars. For what thing is more fragile than the human heart?

The bond between man and bride is private, sacred. But I must tell you, I have learned that a grave fraud is afoot. As if the Featheringtons did not have enough to be dealing with, Miss Marina Thompson is with child and has been from the very first day she arrived in our fair city.

Desperate times may call for desperate measures, but I would wager many will think her actions beyond the pale. Perhaps she thought it her only option, or perhaps she knows no shame. But I ask you, can the ends ever justify such wretched means?

Oh dear. Abigail picked up her skirt and rushed towards the Bridgerton household.

Once there, she knocked on the door, well acquainted with the staff by now so that they simply let her inside and took her gloves and purse. She held onto both the letter and the gossip sheet, and proceeded directly to the dining room where, apparently, only Lady Bridgerton sat.

"Violet, I'm so sorry to rush in." She said as she moved towards her.

"Of course, dear. Are you alright? You didn't return after—"

"I'm fine, I had to take care of some things, but you need to see this."

She pushed the copy of Whistledown into her hands and watched as her expression morphed into one of mild horror.

"Oh my." She whispered and stood from her chair.

She moved around the table and swiftly made her way out of the room. Abigail followed, but stayed in the doorway and watched as Colin made his way down the stairs. Violet stood at the bottom and waited

"What is it?" Colin asked as his pace slowed upon seeing his mother.

She said nothing and simply handed him the gossip sheet. He set down his bags and took it. Now, Abigail watched as his expression also morphed into one of shock. He looked up at his mother, then at the sheet, and then back up again, tears welling in his eyes. Almost immediately, he turned and ran back up the stairs.

As his figure retreated, Anthony entered through the doorway into the house. He took in the room and walked over to his mother where they had a hushed conversation. Abigail only assumed they were talking about Colin and Marina, as the eldest Bridgerton looked up at where Colin had just run from. His mother patted his shoulder and gracefully made her own way up the stairs, no doubt to console her son.

Anthony stood there for a moment, before finally looking over in her direction. Upon fully seeing her, he made a quick movement and walked past her into the dining room, grabbing her wrist to effectively make her follow.

Abigail thought he would speak about what had just happened with Colin, but she would be wrong.

"You said you would come home after talking with your father."

His words were tense and full of concern.

"Technically, I was home."

"Not what I meant. This home." He gestured to the house around him.

She'd never admit it, but this made her heart swell.

"I had some family affairs to get in order." She said in a way of explanation.

"You have to tell me these things. I refuse to have a relationship where we don't talk to each other."

She quirked her brow.

"Have you had a letter from Daphne?"

"Hastings."

"Ah." She paused before making a slight joke. "You don't, by chance, have any secret vows or grudges that will affect our marriage, do you?"

At this he finally laughed and pretended to think for a moment.

"Well, I'd have to think about that."

She gawked and playfully hit his arm. He caught her hand and pulled her close. They wouldn't be able to stay like that for long but it was still nice for the moment.

"We'll be just fine." She assured him as well as herself.

Chapter 27

Miss Marina Thompson's recent fall from grace continues to echo through every drawing room in town, days after it was revealed her engagement to Colin Bridgerton was nothing more than a sham. Of course, a lady's disgrace does not merely tarnish her own name. Like the tars of the Thames, it also leaves a horrid   smear   on   anyone
n   e   a   r   -
by.

   "Hold still, ma chérie." Madame Delacroix instructed, as Eloise could not stop fidgeting.

   "This scandal could very well tarnish my debut, Mama. Perhaps we should delay my coming out altogether a few years."

   "Oh hush, child, all will be well. Just keep smiling."

   Abigail glanced up and caught Lady Richmond and a few others casting nervous glances towards them.

"Can a smile be enough to save the Featheringtons? Penelope and her sisters did nothing wrong, but their reputations are destroyed."

"You should be worrying about your own family's fortunes at present. We are in just as perilous a position." Lady Bridgerton warned her in a hush tone only mothers seemed to be capable of using.

"But—"

"Time and place, El." Abigail muttered to Eloise before she could protest any further.

"Lovely day, is it not, Lady Richmond?" Violet called, receiving only a forced smile and a nod in return.

Well, we can't have that.

"Oh goodness Lady Richmond, is that you?" Abigail stepped forward, putting on a sweet tone that was just believable enough.   "Oh Miss Bentley, hello." She nodded and attempted to go back to her fabrics.

Now near her, Abigail continued, not allowing her to end the conversation.

"I cannot believe it. I was just thinking of you. My mother used to tell me that if there was anyone who could elegantly accessorize, it was you."

Abigail prayed she would take the bait and not catch on to the fact that she was blatantly buttering her up. Thankfully, she didn't notice.

"Well, really?" The woman asked, seemingly flattered.

"Why, yes! I remember, she admired your broach, the one with the circlet of pearls and sapphires. I confess I have found myself admiring it at several events this season, myself." She added a small laugh that would have sounded so dainty and fake to anyone who knew her, but Lady Richmond didn't seem to notice.

"Oh, your mother was a dear. In fact, it's funny you should mention the broach because it was a gift passed from my great great..."

Mission accomplished. The woman kept talking about the broach that Abigail knew she was far too proud of; precisely why she had mentioned it. In all honesty, her mother had never spoken of Lady Richmond, but Abby had overheard her at several functions boasting about the piece, so as she knew it would be a safe choice of conversation.

"...he swore he bought it off of the pirate Bartholomew Roberts, have you ever heard such a thing?"

Abigail forced a laugh.

"I could never imagine." She glanced behind her where Madame Delacroix was finishing hemming Eloise's dress. "Well, we really must be off. Lady Bridgerton?" She called.

"Ah, yes Abigail, darling." She came and met the women by the fabric's stand, pulling Eloise with her.

"Well, we will see you soon. You will be at the Opera next week, will you not?" Abigail questioned, a smile still plastered on her face.

"Why yes, we will see you all there." Lady Richmond confirmed. "Miss Bentley, Lady Bridgerton." She nodded her head at them both and they walked their separate ways.

Once back in the carriage, Violet broke the silence.

"Is that true, about your mother?"

"Of course not. But we all know her affection for that piece of jewelry." Abigail confirmed with a wink towards Eloise. And if she wasn't mistaken, she saw a sort of proud smile appear on Violet's face.

While there is no parasol in the world strong enough to shelter a ruined woman, the fallen Miss Thompson can only hope she shall find a refuge... somewhere.

"Miss Thompson must be in agonies over these lies. Why can I not visit her?" Colin protested from his spot, standing in the parlor.

All the Bridgerton men were about the parlor with Abigail and Violet each on a couch opposite each other. Abigail attempted to leave earlier, understanding this was a family situation, but Colin had stopped her. He insisted she was the only one who had ever been kind to him about his engagement with Marina, and he wanted her there. Plus, after the display at the modiste that day, Violet insisted she stay as well.

"Colin—" Violet started but was interrupted.

"Listen to me, brother. That the ton devours every bit of Whistledown's on-dis is the only thing keeping this family from shame. Because of her column, no one believes you are the father of Miss Thompson's child. But if you are to go near her, then they will presume you responsible for her ruin, and all your sisters will pay the price for your notoriety." Anthony finished explaining in the most condescending way possible. "Is this what you desire?"

"Well of course not, but—"

Now he was interrupted, this time by the door opening. It was Daphne, and while she technically looked fine, something about her seemed off, strained even.

"Evening, everyone."

"Dearest!" Violet, exclaimed and stood.

"What are you doing here, Daph? Should you not be frolicking in newlywed bliss?" Anthony questioned from behind Abigail's couch.

"I came as swiftly as our carriage would allow when I heard the news. Oh, Abby hello!" She made a beeline for Abigail, pulling her up and into a hug, to which Abby gratefully reciprocated.

"You left in the middle of your honeymoon?" Anthony questioned further.

"Hastings must surely be cursing the Bridgerton name for this." Benedict joked.

Though he said it light-heartedly, it was clear Daphne did not take it so.

"Where is he, anyhow?"

"He went to set up Hastings House." She replied, simply.

"We have all things in order sister, we do not require your assistance." Anthony insisted.

Abby finally chimed in, turning slightly to see him.

"Well that is simply not true, and you know it. Daphne may be the answer to all of our problems."

Anthony gave her an annoyed look to which she replied with one of her own. It was fascinating, they weren't even married yet and they still were managing silent communication.

"Abigail is right. Once the ton sees that we still have the favor of the Duke and Duchess, then the whispers may very well cease, and we shall go about our daily lives as if nothing has happened. As if nothing is awry." Violet looked pleased once again.

"And no one will be the wiser." Daphne added, barely hiding the bitterness apparent in her tone. "Pretending

that nothing is amiss is the perfect way to lure the igno-
rant into submission. Is it not, Mama?"

Violet looked taken aback, evidently not understanding what Daphne was referring to. But Abigail thought
she had a pretty good idea.

"Now, what grand event will the ton be descending
upon this week? Surely there is something." Daphne
changed the subject.

Violet cleared her throat, still off guard.

"The uh... The Queen is hosting a luncheon."

"I am certain the Duke and I can secure an invitation.
If we are lucky, our return to London will give everyone
so much to talk about they simply will have no breath
left to discuss other matters."

Finally, Colin piped up, angry.

"I'm so very glad this has all been settled on my be-
half." And with that, he stormed off, slamming the door
on his way out.

Daphne spared a glance around the room and swiftly
followed him out. Soon, Benedict followed and only Anthony, Abigail and Violet were left in the room.

With her mind in other places, Abigail nearly jumped
when she felt Anthony's hand softly rest on her shoulder. Reaching subconsciously for it, she looked back and
met his eyes. They flitted forward to his mother and
back to her. Understanding the message, she looked

over towards Violet, who was clearly lost in her own thoughts, then met Anthony's gaze once more and nodded.

"Um, Violet." She began, gently, catching her attention. "I know you have quite a bit on your mind at the moment, but I have something to tell you... um..." She looked towards Anthony who was making his way round the couch.

"Actually, we have something to tell you. You might want to sit."

And so she did. Anthony sat as well, next to Abby.

"It's like this..." Abby started, but trailed off, not knowing how to go about it.

"Mother, a short while ago I asked for Abigail's hand."

He slipped his left one into her right and she instantly felt comfort wash over her.

"And I accepted." She finished.

They both sat there, waiting. For some reaction, any reaction. But the woman stayed still. In fact, her eyes had wandered off, no longer looking at either of them. Anthony and Abby both exchanged glances, not knowing if this was good or bad.

Just about when Abigail was going to say something else, Violet let out a laugh. A large, joyous and boisterous laugh. She covered her mouth with her hands and shut her eyes, as if praying this were true.

"Oh thank God." She finally said. "Anthony had been on my list of worries for a very long time and... oh! This is just wonderful!" She stood up and went to hug her son first. "Oh I'm so happy for you my dear." She whispered to him, then turned to his fiancé. "For both of you." And she immediately met Abby in a hug as well.

Abigail felt everything at once: warmth, joy, and most of all relief. This was the best possible reaction they could have hoped for.

"But, oh, I'm sorry. We'll have to wait until this whole scandal blows over, but then we can finally announce it. In the meantime, we'll tell the family tomorrow. Oh this is just what I needed!"

Violet then left the room, still laughing. And once she could be heard no more, Anthony and Abigail turned towards each other. Both still looked stunned, but then, much like Violet's reaction, they burst into laughter. Anthony immediately swooped down and swept her off the floor, spinning around. This was going to happen, finally.

Chapter 28

"**C**olin, you have to take a breath... and maybe stand still for a moment." Abigail suggested lightly.

He stopped pacing around the grand parlor of Hastings House. She, Colin and Daphne were waiting for Miss Thompson to arrive. Truthfully, Abigail wasn't sure why she was there, but Colin had asked, and she'd do anything for him at the moment.

Abigail walked through the foyer of the Bridgerton house that morning, the foyer she had grown rather fond of, and made her way towards the dining room. She caught sight of Colin stepping off the stairs and called his name, effectively catching his attention. Once next to him, she lowered her volume, not quite sure how to approach the subject.

"Look, um, we told your mother last night, about Anthony and I, and she asked that we tell the family this morning." She sighed. "If you don't wish to come in right now, I completely understand."

Colin gave her a sad smile.

"You are perhaps the only person who's stopped to consider my point of view in all this. Anthony's lucky. Honest to God, I think you're too good for him." She laughed at this and he paused for a moment before saying, "I am happy for you, Abby, I just—"

"I know. It's perfectly alright."

He began to walk away from the dining room, and she moved towards it, but then his voice stopped her, and she turned around.

"Abigail, I am going to Hastings House today. Daphne has managed for me to have a chaperoned conversation with Marina. And well, I don't know if you have plans but Daphne just doesn't understand and..." he trailed off.

"I'll be there, if you'd like me to."

He looked relieved and continued to walk away. Finally, she turned and successfully walked into the dining room.

"Ah, to what do we owe this surprise?" Benedict asked upon her entrance.

"Abby! Are you joining us for breakfast?" Hyacinth piped up in an excited tone.

Before she could reply, a voice, and a very handsome one at that, spoke from behind her.

"She isn't the only one." Sure enough, Anthony came but next to her.

"Anthony!" This time, the exclamation came from Gregory.

"Alright... what is happening here?" Eloise asked, a tone of suspicion in her voice.

The couple at the head of the table exchanged glances, Anthony not bothering to hide his smile. The smile that was, admittedly, infectious.

"Perhaps we should wait for your mother—" Abigail began.

"No need, I'm just here." Violet entered, smiling.

"What is going on?" Eloise repeated the question, her tone becoming impatient.

Abigail looked up towards Anthony.

"It is either you or me." She said in a low tone.

He smirked and slipped his arm around her waist.

"Everyone, I have asked Abigail for her hand in marriage, and for some outlandish reason she has accepted."

Unlike the reaction they had experienced the previous night, almost the second the words had left Anthony's mouth everyone in the dining room stood and cheered. Hugging and congratulations began immediately.

"Oh Abby, you're going to be my sister!" Hyacinth was heard from where she clung around the debutant's waist.

"I would've thought you had enough." Abigail joked and hugged the youngest Bridgerton back.

"I'm just happy to have someone around who appreciate's my point of view." Eloise squeezed in a hug once Hyacinth had released Abigail.

"Oh yes because you are so oppressed." Anthony's sarcastic comment was heard on their left.

Abigail turned and arched her brow, effectively silencing him. Benedict, who was next to his brother, gave a laugh at the interaction.

"Are we sure you two aren't already married?"

Before either of them could clip back however Hyacinth butted in with yet another question.

"Oh! Are you two going to live here now?"

Furrowing her brows, Abigail realized they hadn't discussed this at all. With all of their difficulties simply trying to announce the engagement, they hadn't once discussed what happened next. But by the looks of it, Anthony had.

"I believe we'll spend some time in my lodgings before we can all discuss what's best for everyone's living situation. I would never want to uproot anyone."

Abigail smiled, but on the inside she was debating whether to admire his thoughtfulness or be irritated she had made this decision without consulting her. Obviously she wouldn't say anything now, however something inside her said the subject would be revisited.

Abigail's thoughts drifted back from the memories of this morning and came back down to reality as Miss Thompson entered the room.

"Ah, Miss Thompson." Daphne greeted her, all the life that used to coat her voice seemed to be gone, leaving behind an oddly formal, and oddly stiff version of her best friend. "Thank you for joining us."

"I did not realize I had a choice." Marina's harsher tone cut through the air.

"My brother wished for an audience. And I wish to avoid any further scandal attached to my family's name." She looked between them and said, "I will remain here as a chaperone, and Abigail will sit with me, to keep me company, as well as to keep us all sane."

Abigail smiled slightly and gave Marina a sympathetic nod. She wasn't pleased with the circumstances she'd put her soon to be in-laws in, however, she found it rather difficult to completely blame her. What was she to do as a woman in this society? Her options were either to get rid of the child and die trying, or find a man who would cherish her and the baby. She would never voice this opinion to anyone, but she had a strange sense that Colin knew she felt that way, maybe that's why he wanted her here.

She and Daphne took a seat next to each other, across the room, giving the illusion of privacy to the couple. Abby took up a bit of needlework and Daphne gathered a book in her hands.

"Marina... you must tell me that this Whistledown woman is mistaken. What she wrote cannot be true." Colin's voice seemed to be breaking already.

"But it is."

"You are... with child?"

Though she and Daphne were not looking, Abby knew Marina was nodding.

"I do not understand. We were to be wed. You... you said you loved me."

"Colin, I hold you in the greatest esteem."

"Esteem?" He repeated. "You are a cruel woman indeed to stand here and talk of friendly affection, as if you have not just committed a grave sin against me."

"Speak not of sin, Mr. Bridgerton." Marina's words became cold. "I did not come here to be shamed by you, nor anyone else." She sent a look towards Abigail and Daphne who were, rather conspicuously watching them.

They looked back down.

Marina took a long moment before she spoke again.

"I did not know better. You may think me a villain, but I did what I thought I must. No one ever truly helped me, or guided me in a different direction. I had no choice." She took a breath. "I needed to wed. And you, you were the only man who offered me even a glimpse of happiness."

"So I should feel flattered then?" It was almost as if Colin's heart was breaking, right there on the parlor floor. "Consider myself lucky that you chose me, lied to me, tried to trick me into a fraud of a marriage?"

Abigail's peripheral vision fought Daphne's grip tighten around her book as well as her breath sharpen.

Colin stepped forward rather formally.

"I shall take my leave of you for the last time, Miss Thompson." He began to walk towards the door but stopped with his hand on the doorknob.

Turning back around, he said, "You wish to know the cruelest part of your deception? If you had simply come to me and told me of your situation... I would have married you without a second thought. That is how 'in love' I believed myself to be. But I see now that was all a lie." With that he stormed out.

Marina stood, looking at the spot where he left with a look of shock and shame written on her face. Abigail supposed she should be shocked, most men would not have offered to marry an already pregnant woman, but Colin wasn't 'most men'. In fact, Abigail knew for a fact all of the Bridgerton men would have reacted the same way for someone they cared for. It was a comforting knowledge, indeed.

There were several moments silence before Daphne moved forward in an attempt to approach Marina. However, she didn't get very far.

"I believe I would like to return home now. After all, we don't want another scandal attached to your family name." She sounded bitter. But, then again Abigail supposed she had every right to sound so.

Daphne stared into space with a look of deep thought as Marina walked out. Before Abigail could inquire as to what those thoughts were, however, Rose came in and announced that the carriage was waiting and they must prepare for The Queen's luncheon.

Chapter 29

T he Queen's luncheon was less of a luncheon and more of a garden gala. Complete with a string quartet playing while everyone chattered and visited amongst the fully-bloomed gardens. It looked like a scene from a painting, very picturesque.

"Well isn't this lovely?" Abigail heard Violet say from where she stood, on Anthony's arm in the back of the brood that was the Bridgertons. Violet was at the front. "All of us together again. And with some new additions." She nodded to Abigail and the Duke.

While Abby understood what Violet was getting at, she couldn't help but cringe on the inside as she knew the situation was far from lovely. For most of the Bridgertons, yes, it was exciting, but for Colin this had to have been dreadful. Not to mention Abigail was still trying to determine what kept Daphne from acting so un-Daphne-like.

"Lovely indeed, we should tempt scandal more often." Colin's tone was still raw and bitter from earlier this afternoon.

Two women, along with apparently the rest of the ton approached them all, but more specifically Daphne and Simon. Everyone was practically crooning to talk to, or even simply see the new Duke and Duchess back from their honeymoon.

Yet, Abigail wasn't listening to what was being said ahead of them. She was too busy watching Daphne's stiff shoulders and strained smile. Too busy deciphering what could have happened at Clyvdon to put Daphne in such a state of mind.

"I wish I knew what was happening inside your head." It was Anthony's voice that startled her out of her thoughts.

Chuckling at herself, she noticed his hand had made its way around her waist. A rather bold move considering they were in public without having announced the engagement. But there seemed to be enough people preoccupied with the Duke and Duchess to keep them safe.

"My head isn't always a place you'd like to be." She commented, offhandedly.

"What were you thinking about?" He questioned, a concerned tone now laced in his voice.

"I am just worried about..." realizing Daphne might not want to share her troubles with her entire family, she changed courses, "Your brother." She nodded to Colin.

"He'll live." Anthony gave a rather disgruntled sigh.

"Anthony, have you given a moment's thought to what he must be going through?"

"Of course I have, but everyone has been lied to before. It is awful but we overcome it."

She took a long, deep breath, thinking of how she could phrase her point.

"So, if I told you, right now, that I was with child. That I had been with another man, and that everything that had passed between us had only been to get you to marry me, you would be unaffected?"

He furrowed his brows and there was a long moment's pause before he looked her in the eyes.

"You make me a better person, do you know that?"

She laughed.

"It's what wives are supposed to do, so I'm told."

"I do not know how you manage to feel what everyone else is feeling."

Abby simply shrugged.

"I just pay attention, that's all."

He gave her waist a squeeze, which she supposed was his substitute for a kiss as they were in the middle of the palace gardens.

"Would you like some champagne?"

"I would love some."

Anthony left to find either a table or a footman and Abigail looked around, now noticing the crowd had dispersed and the Bridgeton's had separated. Noticing a maze to her left, she entered it, wanting to hopefully escape the mindless chit chat of the ton inside the hedges.

As she walked she could hear the distinct voices of Daphne and Violet up ahead. Not wanting to eavesdrop, she slowed, but she couldn't quite get her body to turn around. Daphne's voice was near shouting now and Abby could hear her, plain as day.

"If you had informed me about the things that were truly important, if I'd have known the truth, then perhaps I—" Daphne's words came to a halt.

Still around the corner, Abigail couldn't see why but she could hear footsteps coming her way. She stayed utterly still, unsure of what to do, it wasn't too absurd for her to be in the maze, but then again she was alone.

That point was moot, however, because when the said footsteps rounded the corner, it was only Daphne. She was crying, or rather trying not to. Yet once she saw Abby, her best friend, her only comfort at the moment, she broke.

Daphne broke down crying, trying to keep quiet for the sake of the entire ton being only a few yards away. Nevertheless, she collapsed in Abby's arms and embraced her in a hug as they both sank to their knees. For the first time in her life, apart from when her mother died, Abigail didn't know what to do.

She always had a solution, a plan. And now, she was rendered speechless. She simply whispered calming words in Daphne's ear as they sat there on the grass, attempting to comfort her best friend in the whole world the best way she could. She just hoped it would be enough.

Chapter 30

♥

Abigail sat in Anthony's study with two candles burning on either side of her. She was still dressed in her clothing from dinner, but her gloves had long since been abandoned, and her caramel hair had been removed from its intricate braid and now hung loosely over her right shoulder.

She probably shouldn't have been in there, but she doubted anyone would know. Everyone had gone to bed at this point. Well, almost everyone. Abby suspected Eloise was reading by candlelight in her bedroom, and Anthony had announced he was going to visit Hastings at their club.

In truth, Abigail had honestly tried to work at the desk in her guest bedroom, or as Hyacinth had taken to calling it: Abby's room, but she found she had no idea what estate accounts were even supposed to look like and she needed an example.

It had occurred to her two days prior that she had no idea what was happening with the accounts and bookings of the Bentley household; and, seeing as she had shipped her father to the country, that had to be her worry now. So, yesterday she had retrieved the many papers from her father's desk and had since been attempting to fix the long overdue work.

The problem was, however, that though she was far from stupid, mathematics had never been a strong point in her schooling. As this was the case, a large brandy from her fiancé's stash also sat in front of her, easing at least some of the stress.

Just as she considered throwing her quill across the room, a scraping noise interrupted her thoughts and actions. Looking up, she saw Anthony with his hand still on the doorknob, evidently he was just as surprised to see her.

"What are you doing in here?" She questioned rising from her seat... well, his seat.

"I could ask you the same question." He stepped closer toward her and the candlelight, and that's when she took in a breath.

"What happened?" She picked up the closest candle to inspect the large cut down the side of his right eye.

He sighed and seemingly braced himself.

"I might have gotten into a tuft with Hastings."

"You hit your brother-in-law?"

"Well, as you can see it wasn't one sided."

"You know what, I'm not even going to question at the moment, just sit and I'll fetch some water and a cloth."

He didn't protest as he moved to sit in his big leather chair she had just recently vacated. She, meanwhile, took her candle and ran to the dining room, hoping the linens and a water pitcher would be there, as they normally were. She was right.

Returning, she set the jug and the linens down, and moved to sit on the desk in front of him. She held the candle closer and winced as she saw how deep the cut actually went.

"It's really not that bad." He tried to assure her.

"Says you."

She reached for her brandy glass and took her last sip before dipping the cloth in it.

"What are you— ah!" He protested in pain as she applied the alcohol to the wound.

"Sorry but it's the only thing in the room that will stop an infection."

He didn't respond, instead he took the brandy glass from her hand and finished the rest in one large swig.

"Well that's one way to numb the pain." She chuckled, now having the water cloth in her hand.

Again, he didn't say anything and simply snaked his hands around her waist and pulled her down to sit on his lap.

She acknowledged this action with a smile but stayed focused on her task, wiping away more and more blood. She watched his eyes flit away from her and back to the papers on his desk, behind her.

"May I ask what you were working on in my study?"

"Nothing." She said, almost in reflex.

His hand at her hip tugged, and she looked in his eyes. He gave her an incredulous look.

"Sorry, I suppose it's just become such a habit to defend suspicion around my family." She gave the apology and moved back to his cut.

He looked around her again and finally spoke again.

"Are you... settling accounts?"

She took a long, deep breath and set the cloth down.

"I'm trying to, but making rather a mess of it." She admitted.

"Abigail," He started, and she noticed his use of her full name. He hadn't used it hardly ever since they'd become engaged. "I know you do not like to talk about him much, but why isn't your father doing this?"

She gave a dry laugh that resembled no humor whatsoever.

"Because I've sent him away to the country, remember? Though in total fairness he had been neglecting these long before then."

"How are you... well, how are you doing?" He seemed hesitant to ask.

She paused before tumbling out a response.

"Awfully, I'm afraid. I know I am capable, but I haven't been taught how to do any of this. It seems as though God himself wants me to fail, and I know if I could only understand the numbers and the symbols I would actually be able to keep our estates in order for Ben and Cal, but at this rate they will be simply left to fend for themselves because I—"

"Woah! Woah... hey. It's alright, breath." Interrupting, he put a calming hand on her cheek to hopefully sooth the upcoming panic attack.

"I— I can't do this." She was breathing hard and close to tears now.

"I can help you, if you'd like." His voice was the one calming thing in the storm.

"Anthony, that's— that's very sweet but my family's burdens should not be your burdens."

"Yes they bloody well should." He moved his hand under her chin and forced her to look at him. "We're getting married, Abby, and I couldn't be happier about it."

She smiled and let out a breathy laugh as she leaned her forehead against his.

"Plus," he added. "You seem to take on all of my family's problems, it's about time I helped with yours."

Chapter 31

♥

Abigail gently twisted the knob on the door to Eloise's bedroom. She knew Violet was helping her get ready, and the last thing Abby wanted to do was intrude. Yet still, she felt the need to talk to her soon to be sister-in-law before they left for the concert. Call it what you want, but she had a strange sense about Eloise's intentions this evening. She wasn't about to accuse Eloise of anything nefarious, and yet she felt a an unexplainable suspicion, and simply had to sway it before   they   all left.

"...we need not hasten your coming out before you feel prepared." She heard Violet finish her sentence as she carefully stepped into the room.

There was a moment's pause in which Eloise simply stared back at her mother.

Finally, she said, "The Queen will be in attendance at tonight's concert will she not?"

"I believe she will."

"Then I am looking forward to it. An exciting time, indeed, mama."

This was as good a moment as any to intrude.

"Sorry to interrupt." Abigail piped up, softly, from her place by the door. "I just wondered if I could borrow some lip brewed off of you, Eloise."

"Of course." She seemed to regain her senses as she removed herself from her spot in front of the mirror, and headed toward her vanity.

"I'll leave you to it, I have to check and make sure Anthony and Benedict are ready." Violet took her leave.

Abigail's eyes followed her as she left the room, and listened for the click of the door behind her.

"Here you are." Eloise pulled her attention back, and held out a tin of rosy paste toward her.

"What are you up to, Eloise?" Abigail didn't even bother to explain herself as she took the tin and got straight to the question.

Shocked, Eloise sputtered and it took several moments before she responded.

"What?"

"Oh please, I know you would rather go to the stake than attend a high society affair. And now, you're suddenly so interested in The Queen's attendance..." She trailed off, leaving her question apparent.

"I believe," Eloise began. "You are the only one who's ever taken the time to notice my true opinions."

"Normally, I'd take that as a compliment, but something's telling me that you wanted to go unnoticed tonight."

"Alright. But if I tell you... promise not to say a word to mama."

"I promise."

"Or Anthony."

She hesitated.

"Ha! I knew you couldn't."

"I didn't say that! I'm rather good with secrets thank you, it's just... we're not even married yet and I'm choosing his sister's side over his." She said that last part more to herself than anyone else.

"Swear. Otherwise, I'm sorry, but you cannot know."

"Alright, I swear."

"Good." Eloise took a long breath before finally saying, "The Queen has tasked me with uncovering Lady Whistledown's identity. I am attending tonight's concert so that I can report to her."

"You mean you've found who she is?" Abigail didn't bother to hide the shock from her voice.

"Not quite, but I do know she is a tradesperson."

"I see..."

Eloise took a moment, gauging Abby's reaction, before continuing.

"Now that you know this... you won't report me to mama?"

Abigail snorted.

"What do you think I am, a tattletale? No this is fairly harmless so I don't see a need to tell anyone. Although I hope when you nail down her identity I will be one of the few to know."

"So you think I can do this?" Eloise sounded in disbelief.

"I think if anyone can, it's you." She simply shrugged as if this was an obvious conclusion. "Now, with that out of the way, how on earth are you going to stand four hours in the midst of a gossiping, inebriated ton?"

Abby moved to the mirror and opened the tin Eloise gave her to apply some of the paste to her lips.

"Four hours? Be serious."

Abby held a glint in her eye as she turned back around.

"Oh I am... which is why we're going to need a plan to keep you sane."

———-

Downstairs, Anthony cautiously entered his study, where Colin stood over a table, adding to his maps.

"Missing the concert?" He announced his arrival.

"Indeed. I'm not exactly in the mood for music and finery this evening." Colin explained, then simply bent his head back over his work.

Anthony said nothing, but simply poured his brother a drink and stalled saying the words he knew he had to.

Extending the drink to Colin he finally said, "I want to apologize."

The younger took the drink, eyeing his brother suspiciously.

"Are there locusts in the streets? Blood in the Thames? Are the end of days upon us already."

Anthony sighed in exasperation, but nevertheless was happy Colin was willing to joke with him.

"I may have been a trifle harsh with you." He admitted.

"And is Abigail the only reason you've come to this conclusion?"

"She may have helped me see what it might have been like in your shoes. And I'm now sorry for the way I have acted."

"You merely wished to protect me from my more... foolish impulses." He cast his eyes down to his drink.

"So you admit it now? You were acting a fool?"

"As apologies go, this is certainly novel."

"Hush, you."

They both chuckled, happy they were back to bickering. Tension gone from the room, they sat on opposite sides of the table.

"You may hurt now but the pain will pass. You have the love of all your family, and the honor of your actions. Soon you will forget Miss Thompson's name and it will..." he sighed and trailed off. He knew what he was going to say but then changed courses. "Let's be honest, she will probably always be painful in your memory, but later you will find someone who makes the pain dull, and it will almost be as if you never loved her at all."

"You sound as if you've already met that someone. I do hope we're thinking of the same woman."

Anthony chuckled, but he couldn't suppress the grin that came about when he thought of her. It was almost as if he had no control over himself. Thinking of her caused elation, joy... something that words couldn't quite describe.

"Honest to God, I don't know what she sees in me sometimes."

"None of us do."

Anthony gasped in mock anger and tossed a crumpled paper across the table at him.

"Everything alright in here?" They both heard the woman they were speaking of from the doorway.

She was dressed in a soft gold and the candlelight made the jewels attached to her neck sparkle. Good God, she was a vision

"Better than, actually." Colin responded. "Anthony actually admitted fault."

"And no one's died of the plague yet?"

Colin burst out laughing while Anthony proceeded to roll his eyes.

"Oh, Ha. Ha." He finally gulped down the last of his drink and stood, his eyes now fixed on Abigail.

Before he could ask her if they were all ready, however, Eloise's voice came sounding throughout the downstairs.

"Abby! Please don't tell me I have to wear this blasted tiara all night!"

Abigail stayed facing forward and didn't even flinch as she called back.

"Yes, I'm afraid you do!"

"Oh, why don't you just kill me then."

Snorting, Abby reached for Anthony's hand and laced her fingers through his to drag him out the room.

"Well, it's a good thing we're not dramatic."

They both joined everyone in the foyer, and saw Violet fussing over something in Eloise's hair while the daughter in question simply kept swatting her hand away.

"Right." Anthony announced to try and interrupt before someone burst. "Everyone ready?"

"I believe so." Violet finally pulled away from her second daughter and assessed everyone in the room. "Let's be off then."

Eloise and Benedict headed to the doorway, and Abigail made to follow before Anthony caught her arm, efficiently stopping her. Although he didn't say a word to her, he simply stepped forward to whisper something she couldn't hear in his mother's ear. To which Violet only nodded and smiled.

"What was—" Abby started to question before Anthony had shushed her and pulled her arm forward.

Abigail watched as Benedict and Eloise were herded into one of the carriages by Violet before she stepped in herself, leaving the second one just completely free for the two of them.

"Why did she—"

"You ask too many questions." She could hear the smile in his voice. "Come on."

Anthony gave another tug and, in record time, she was seated in the other carriage straight across from him.

"Anthony, what are you doing?" She couldn't quite stop herself from asking another question.

"This." He said as he reached for something in his pocket.

The carriage started to move and Abigail had to reach to the side to steady herself as she leaned forward, towards her fiancée.

From his pocket, Anthony pulled a small, square, velvet box and held it out to her. Taking it, her heart racing as she did so, she stared at the thing in her hands before finally opening the lid. She took in a deep breath, so as to stop herself from gasping.

Inside the jewelry box laid a small, rather simple gold band, and on it a single round-cut diamond. The gem stone seemed to sparkle in the fading light from the window of the carriage, and Abby soon found she could not take her eyes off it.

"Anthony it's-- it's beautiful." She smiled and looked up at him.

"May I?" He prompted and reached his hand out for her own.

She extended her left hand and felt her heartbeat quicken even more as he delicately undid the fingers of her glove and slid the satin off. She was sure he could tell her breathing was out of control, but she didn't care. All that mattered was him. All that seemed to exist was him.

"It's a Bridgerton heirloom. There are several in the collection, as you can imagine, but I thought you'd like this one."

He slid it onto her finger and she couldn't deny how very safe she felt. Excited, on fire, and utterly in love as well, but very safe.

"I love it. Thank you."

"I'm sorry it's taken me so long, we've had some... things going on."

At this, they both burst into laughter. If this could be titled an easy courtship, she didn't want to see a difficult one.

"It's perfect." She finally said. "You're perfect."

That last part she whispered, but in the confined space of the carriage he heard it as if she'd shouted.

He couldn't control himself any longer. He wasted no time in leaning forward, capturing her lips with his and keeping her there. Seeing her like this, feeling her like this. It made him so happy, to a heart-swelling, somewhat nauseating degree. But he wouldn't have any other way.

Chapter 32

"Then where did you meet her?" Eloise's voice closely followed the quick pace of Benedict's footsteps.

"About town." He responded, curtly.

"At her shop?"

"Should you not be off somewhere getting ready to attend your very first ball?"

He really said it just to shut her up, but if he thought this would work, then he didn't know his sister. For she simply dove further into pestering him.

"What other places might she frequent besides her shop?"

Abigail's voice cut through the conversation before Benedict could scream the reply he so obviously was preparing.

"El, leave alone what business isn't yours. If you're desperate for something to occupy your mind, you could certainly help me over here."

Abigail occupied almost half the drawing room, surrounded by a multitude of papers and servants. All morning she had been answering questions pertaining to guests, floral arrangements, and menus. And in total honesty, she was not enjoying herself. Oh sure, she originally believed it would be fun but that was before she truly started, and realized simply how much needed to get done in the mere two weeks before her wedding day. In truth, she was drowning.

"Yes, leave me alone and help Abigail with the women's work." He had settled on the other side of the drawing room with his sketchbook and seemed in immense relief at Abby's suggestion.

"Do not make me regret helping you, Benedict." Her tone quickly shifted to a warning one as she had little patience to begin with. "I could just as easily make you come and help me with all this."

Before he could reply however, Anthony entered the room. Attention shifted toward him, and his siblings noticed how he seemed to relax the instant he laid eyes on his fiancé.

"So this is why I haven't seen you for nearly two days." He was half kidding, half complaining.

Eloise and Benedict simply looked at each other in amusement. He was already a completely changed man from the one they had known nearly a month ago. Eloise went back to whispering her annoying inquiries about Madame Delacroix, while the couple continued their own conversation.

Abigail gave Anthony an apologetic look and set down one of the stacks of papers she was holding.

"Well, I'm about to take a break for some tea, would you care to join me?"

Before he could reply in the affirmative however, Daphne poked her head into the room. She looked paler than normal and rather melancholy, though it was quite obvious she was trying to hide it. Well, maybe not obvious to everyone, but Abigail noticed.

"Ah, Abby. I was just about to go into town and I want to hear all about your wedding preparations. Would you join me?"

"Oh, no." Anthony interrupted before Abby could reply. "This is my fiancé and I haven't seen her in days."

His voice held an air of finality, and with most people, it would have worked. But this was not most people, this was his sister.

"Well, she was my best friend first, and I haven't seen her in over a week so, I win." Daphne gave him a triumphant look and walked into the room just to take Abigail's wrist and pull her out.

"Oh, alright, I guess I'm going with you now." Abby muttered in minor confusion as she was pulled out of the room.

She cast one more apologetic glance at Anthony before she lost sight of him and headed down the stairs with Daphne.

"Okay, Daph I'm coming, you can let go now."

"Oh, sorry." She let go of her friend as they reached the doorway.

Abigail reached for her gloves and coin purse from Olivia, who was waiting next to Rose for them to come down.

After they got out of the door and down the steps, Abigail finally asked what she had been wanting to for weeks.

"So, what's wrong?"

"What makes you think something's wrong?" Daphne's response was almost automatic.

She simply responded with an arched brow, knowing her best friend better than that.

"I'm sorry, you're right."

And before either of them quite knew what was happening, Daphne was relenting everything that had happened since her marriage to Simon. She told her about his insistence that he couldn't have children, about how Daphne had been kept in the dark, about their lack of speaking, and just about when she reached her failed pregnancy, they had made it to the market.

Several moments of silence passed between them as Abigail digested all the recent information. It was, truly, a lot to get in a quarter of an hour.

Finally, Abigail only had one thing to say.

"Now that you know you are not pregnant," She reached and gave her friend's hand a sympathetic squeeze. "What are you two going to do now?"

"I have made my decision. The Duke and I are going our separate ways."

Abigail sighed and simply shook her head.

"It is for the best, truly." Daphne tried to assure her.

Abby tightened her grip on Daphne's hand and pulled her aside. Out of the line of traffic that automatically came from being in the market.

"I know I have yet to wed and truly have no leg to stand on when I tell you this; but however difficult forgiving him may be, it is necessary to move forward."

"That is not up to me, Abby." Daphne responded, sounding spiteful. "The Duke is choosing to nurture some grudge against his father instead of allowing himself any kind of happiness. However am I supposed to forgive that? However are we supposed to move forward from there?"

Abby only shook her head further.

"I will not pretend to be in your position. But Daphne, you and I have only known what loving households are like. I cannot even begin to imagine how deep Simon's resentment towards his father goes. Does it excuse his behavior? No. But my guess is he doesn't even realize how much he is stopping himself from."

Daphne stayed silent at this. She looked contemplative and Abby, realizing this could go on for a while, linked their arms together and started back on the market path.

"How is it you are able to see so much about another person?" Daphne finally asked.

"I don't know, really. I've always simply just left my own shoes and put myself into someone else's. Anthony says I spend so much time in other people's shoes, I forget I have my own." She added with a chuckle.

"My brother was lucky to have found you." Said Daphne.

Before Abigail could reply that it was the other way round, Lady Featherington seemed to approach them from out of nowhere.

"Your Grace? I do hope you are finding everything you need for Friday's ball. It will certainly be the event of the season. Of course, my young ladies will have to hear about the wondrous festivities the next day, seeing how they did not receive an invitation."

Well she had made her point clear. Yet, it wasn't like Mrs. Featherington to make a remark tactfully, so she went on.

"Prudence in particular is in tears about it. Is she not, Mrs. Varley?" She turned to her housekeeper.

"Oh! Uh, absolute watering pot, that one."

Abby and Daphne exchanged glances, and Abigail gestured to her, inferring that it was her decision. Personally, she never saw why Penelope and her sisters should have to suffer. But this was not her ball, nor her brother that was heartbroken.

"Well, perhaps we can make room." Daphne said with much grace. "I certainly would have no problem extending my invitation, as I am sure all of us would like to forgive the errors of the past, and move forward."

Abigail smiled, knowing Daphne was making a direct reference to their earlier conversation.

"How wonderful!" Lady Featherington was simply shining with glee.

"Apologies ma'am." Her maid, Varley, interrupted. "But it seems a carriage has arrived back at the house. A 'Mr. Crane' is there."

This caught Daphne's attention, who unwound her arm from Abigail's and stepped forward.

"I beg your pardon, but did you say 'Crane'? Would that be a 'Sir George Crane'?"

Abigail didn't get to hear the rest of the story as Daphne departed company from her, promising she would explain later. As Daphne went off with Mrs. Featherington, Abby was left to her own devices. Knowing she would have to go back to wedding planning if she returned to the house, she decided to just stroll and wander the market for the next hour... or three.

Chapter 33

Abigail walked with a quick pace towards the parlor. The whole family was in there, and while that should be incentive enough, she was desperate to escape the endless questioning about the wedding.

Luck seemed to be on her side as she was close enough to hear the laughter coming from the drawing room. But alas, just as she was about to turn the corner, she was affronted by the housekeeper.

"Ah good, Miss. I need to ask you a couple of things just for a moment—"

"Might it wait? I'm meant to join everyone for the celebration." Abigail desperately attempted to cut her off as she skirted around her.

Almost to the parlor, almost there.

"Very quickly, Miss." Mrs. Wilson just followed her, unaffected by her quickened pace. "Would you prefer your cake soaked in rum or brandy?"

"Brandy, I think." She was crossing the entrance of the doorway now

Everyone's attention turned toward them, it seemed Daphne and Simon had just arrived.

"And would it be bacon or ham with eggs for the ceremony?"

She was going to explode, and it was going to be now. Something on her face or in her posture must have said it because suddenly Anthony's voice came from across the room.

"Ham, I believe. Right, darling?"

He strode over to her and wrapped his arms around her shoulder, while hers automatically found his middle.

"Yes, ham. Lovely." She forced a smile.

Mrs. Wilson simply smiled and gave a slight bow before she left, seemingly unaware of the tension radiating off of the soon to be Viscountess.

She turned and visibly relaxed in Anthony's arms, he just chuckled and kissed the top of her head. While, technically it was considered improper for couples to show affection in the presence of others, this was their family and they certainly weren't going to stop for them.

Although, in hindsight, maybe they should have because as soon as they embraced, a rounding chorus of "Ooooo"'s came from the adjacent Bridgertons.

"Alright." Anthony sighed and regrettably pulled from her, but only so much that they were now holding hands.

"So I am to receive another sister as well. I didn't think Anthony could find anyone mad enough to wed him." The comment came from Francesca, who stood from her position on the piano bench.

"Francesca, good to see you." Abigail said with a chuckle and reached in for a hug.

"Well, before the interruption, Fran was about to show us some of the pianoforte she had learned." Colin had a teasing tone in his voice.

"Oh yes, I'm sorry please continue." Insisted Abigail, decidedly in a more pleasant headspace.

"Well, here's where we're at an impasse, for I only said I would do it if Colin accompanied me."

"Oh you might regret that suggestion, sister."

"Why?" Abigail interjected. "Afraid, Colin?"

"Oh, I see what you did there. Alright, I'll sing." He took the bait.

He began to sing, surprisingly on key, and everyone clapped along as Francesca played the piano keys beautifully. Looking around, Abigail searched her memory for a time when she had ever felt this content. She supposed there must have been a time, but she honestly couldn't remember one.

Chapter 34

"Ah! Abigail, good to see you!" Daphne beamed, noticing her best friend descend the stairs on her brother's arm.

"Oh sure, it's all about Abigail. Now the brother is chopped liver." Anthony's comment could have seemed serious but the sarcasm in his tone betrayed him.

"Welcome in." Simon cut in before Daphne could make another comment.

"Your Graces, thank you for having us." Abigail finally spoke and leaned in to hug Daphne while Anthony reached for Hasting's hand.

"Where's Mama and Eloise? I thought they were coming with you." Daphne questioned.

"They're coming..." Abigail started, not sure how to phrase the rest.

"Eloise had some trouble negotiating with Mother." Anthony finished.

"Of course she did." Daphne rolled her eyes. "Well, it is mostly the same group of people, although I'd steer clear of the southeast corner."

Daphne winked towards Abby and she spared a glance. Sure enough, Cressida and her crones were circling like vultures.

Abigail gave a nod in understanding while Anthony and Simon merely exchanged questioning glances.

"When Daphne and I were younger we used to see who could avoid Cressida Cowper the longest." Abby said in way of explanation.

"I held the record." The Duchess didn't even bother to hide the smug tone in her voice.

"Only because you threw me into the lion's den!"

Before the squabble could continue, however, Colin's voice could be heard approaching them.

"Not to interrupt, but the Duke and Duchess have a small queue forming."

Looking back Abigail noticed the line of guests waiting to be welcomed into the ball.

Anthony gracefully took Abby's arm and said goodbye for the both of them. He pulled his brothers, as well as herself, away.

"Well they seem happier." Abby said, mostly to herself, but forgot who was near her.

"What?" Anthony questioned from beside her, while Benedict added a "What do you mean?"

"Uh, nothing. I-I just knew they were in an argument..."

"What kind of argument?" It was Colin's turn to speak apparently.

They had pulled over to a side of the ballroom and each Bridgerton was staring at her with intensity.

"You know, I am currently realizing that this is most likely not something I should discuss with Daphne's brothers so..." Her eyes scanned for a way out. "Ah, I believe I will visit with Penelope."

Before any of them could protest, she slipped away and was making a beeline for Penelope, she hadn't seen her in ages.

——

So far, the night was turning out to be a huge success. The ballroom, beautifully decorated, was alive with laughter and music. Everyone seemed to be having a grand time. Well, mostly everyone. Eloise looked as if she was ready to keel over at any given moment. Out of boredom or fear no one was sure.

Eloise stood with her brothers and was seriously considering taking up Daphne's offer to use the library, when something caught her attention. Her soon to be sister-in-law was across the room, looking considerably uncomfortable. She was speaking to... oh blast, she couldn't tell. Her height often proved to be a disadvantage.

"Who's that Abigail is talking to?" She voiced her thoughts, interrupting whatever conversation she didn't care about.

"Hm?" Anthony turned to scan the ballroom.

"Over there, near the champagne table."

By now, every Bridgerton brother had their attention directed across the ballroom.

"I believe that's Mr. Twombly. Good God, horrid man" Benedict spoke, being the tallest of them all.

"If you'll excuse me." Anthony made to leave, but was stopped by a hand on his shoulder.

"Not so fast, Bridgerton." Simon had somehow made his way to them. "I've had my fair share of crosses with Twombly, and I don't need a scene made at my wife's ball."

"I will not leave Abby alone with pretentious scum, such as him."

"No need, I believe if your brothers will help me, this could be rather fun."

"Well, I'm certainly not going to miss this." Colin spoke with a bit too much enthusiasm in his voice.

The men made their way across the ballroom and began to hear the conversation being exchanged between Abigail and Mr. Twombly.

"Sir, if you have something to say—"

"I am saying nothing. Just a simple observation that your circumstances have miraculously changed. I mean, it's wonderful, one minute you're alone with a drunken father and the next—"

"Ah, Twombly! We're not threatening people are we?" Simon didn't bother to hide the annoyance in his voice as he approached the conversation with Colin and Benedict.

They all took a spot in the conversation, standing next to Abby, almost like security. It should have felt strange to her, but at the moment she felt so relieved that she didn't have to defend herself and her family again, she decided she was alright with it.

"Uh, Your Grace I can assure you—"

"But of course he was. He's the fourth son of a penny pinching family, he needs to seem more powerful than he actually is." Benedict had lost his coyness as well apparently.

"Excuse me but—"

"Twombly, even in school you were challenging one duel after another. And if anyone thought you were serious, we all knew too well we could have taken you." Simon continued. "I suggest you leave and we won't tell my brother-in-law you were making his fiancé uncomfortable."

Mr. Twombly seemed to receive the message that he was outnumbered. He swallowed and gave a weak smile before walking away.

Abigail let out an audible sigh of relief.

"Horrid man, however did you end up in a conversation with him?" Colin turned toward her.

"I was trying to walk back to you, but he interrupted me." She placed a hand on her forehead, feeling how hot she had become.

Anthony's voice filled her ears and she couldn't have been more grateful.

"Am I allowed to join you now?"

She turned to see him next to her and reached for his hand.

"They wouldn't let me rescue you." He rolled his eyes and pulled her hand up to give it a quick kiss.

"Well, you must admit Bridgerton, this was much more fun." Simon chuckled.

"On that note, thank you for the save." Abby spoke up.

"Anytime. Now if you will excuse me, I believe I have promised a dance with my wife."

They all watched him go and meet Daphne in the middle of the dance floor. They looked happy, or at least completely in love with each other.

As more and more couples joined them, Abigail felt a tug on her hand. Anthony was pulling her onto the floor.

Whatever happened next, during the night or through the rest of her life, couldn't have mattered; because right now, she was completely and incandescently happy.

Chapter 35

♥

"I shall write to you all from Greece." Colin told his family before him from atop his horse. "That is assuming these two actually detach themselves from Midnight."

"Ben! Cal! Come on." Abigail beckoned her two brothers from Colin's steed.

She stood with her new in-laws in front of the Bridgerton house. She and Anthony had married last week and she was in pure, wedded bliss. She didn't know how, but Anthony had managed to get Benjamin and Calvin back from school in time for the wedding. They had both held her hand as she walked down the aisle and as Francesca had said, it was by far the most adorable thing she had ever seen.

They all stood now to see Colin off on his travels, and Ben and Calvin had not left his horse's side since it was brought round.

They came when Abby called, though. Bounding up to where she stood with Anthony, her husband, as she liked to keep reminding herself. Calvin grasped Abby's hand while Benjamin went to stand next to Anthony. In no time, Anthony's arm, the one not entwined around her waist, had made it onto Ben's shoulder.

"Do not forget to bring me a gift." Gregory piped up.

"It is not a gift if you have to ask." Hyacinth scolded. "I would fancy anything blue or white."

Everyone laughed, and Colin simply tipped his hat to them all before riding off.

"Ben, Calvin! Come on, let's play!" Gregory called and the four youngest sprinted off inside the house.

"Well, the two of you are off to Clyvedon now, I presume?"Abigail turned and the couples faced each other.

"We have decided to stay in London a little longer." Simon corrected. "Take some time to enjoy ourselves, just the two of us."

Daphne smiled at him, so clearly in love.

"And you, what are your plans?" She turned and asked them both.

"Oh, we're headed up to Aubrey Hall in Kent. It's been so long since I've seen our country home and well, I'd like some time alone with this one." Anthony turned his head towards Abigail. Who, much to her chagrin, was smiling madly.

<h1 style="text-align:center">Epilogue</h1>

Abigail looked out onto the grounds of her home, Aubrey Hall, thinking about the Whistledown that was delivered that day. Granted, it was a couple of days old seeing as it traveled here by mail from Mayfair, but it proved an interesting read.

It is in silence where one may find truth.

She thought over that line as she added some final flowers to the bouquet in front of her. She had kept silent about this secret for long enough, but she thought she was justified. She needed to be sure, and now that her in-laws were on their way down for the annual Pall-Mall game (or so Anthony called it) she would be able to announce it to everyone at once.

She had arranged for the magnificent yard to be decorated and prepared with tea service, and Anthony had seen to the mallets and wickets.

Speaking of, he should hurry along, his family would be here any minute. She stepped away from the bouquet, and gave one last look over at the table and tent.

"Olivia!" Abby called.

"Yes, Miss." Olivia, her lady's maid, responded from only a few feet away.

"Would you assure that the cakes are put out soon? They should be here any moment."

"Of course, miss."

"And have you seen His Lordship?" Abby added before either of them could move.

"One of the footman said he was in the shed around the corner." Olivia said while giving her mistress a knowing look.

Abigail rolled her eyes. Undoubtedly her husband was trying something to favor his chances of winning later.

She marched along the grounds and around the corner of the estate to find exactly what she expected. Anthony was pulling some wickets out from the shed, and tossing them into two piles.

"What exactly do you think you are doing?" She called

Anthony froze and turned around, an indulgent smirk on his face. He was truly evil. Sometimes he knew just the way to look at her that would turn her knees to liquid.

'Not this time though' she thought to herself, or rather hoped. His family would be here soon, they shouldn't waste time.

"Getting the last few wickets out of storage." He sidled in front of her, his arms automatically finding her waist, and his head ducking down for a kiss.

She swerved, trying to avoid distraction, which was clearly his goal.

Her plan didn't work though. Her husband was too quick and immediately started kissing and sucking on her neck.

Her breath caught.

"Anthony," she bit back a moan as he knew right where her sweet spot was. "Your family will be here any minute."

"You're an excellent Viscountess. Have I ever told you?" He said in between kisses, he was making his way up to her lips. "So smart, dutiful... graceful."

He finally managed to catch her lips and this time she really moaned. It never ceased to amaze her how they could kiss a thousand times and her heart would race just the same as their first.

Practically dragging herself away from his lips, she took a deep breath.

"Flattery might get you far, but it won't work now, grab the wickets and let's go." She put her arms on his chest to physically distance themselves. "I think I hear their carriages."

He grabbed her wrist and yanked her back towards him. She fell into his chest and his hand landed dangerously low.

"Or we could just stay here... maybe go back upstairs... pretend we never left bed this morning." He murmured the last bit into her mouth.

It took several more intoxicating kisses before she pulled back, only slightly, and said the thing that she knew he would respond to.

"Well... I'd be more than happy to oblige, but we'd have to tell your siblings we were forfeiting Pall-Mall first."

This did the trick. As if remembering his scheme with the wickets, he pulled back from her at once, turned to grab the wickets on the left of him, and grabbed her wrist to basically march her back towards the front of their home.

She only laughed. A full, all-encompassing laugh that only the Bridgertons seemed to be able to pull from a person.

They rounded the corner just in time as it seemed. The three carriages holding the Bridgerton tribe, and the Duke and Duchess with little Auggie pulled to a halt, and the footmen began to swiftly unload and open doors. Anthony and Abby both stood, entwined with each other, and waited for the flurry to begin.

It began almost at once. The Viscount and Viscountess were greeted with several hugs, kisses and even an adorable giggle from the baby in Daphne's arms.

"Welcome back, all of you." Abby finally said once they began to settle. "I've laid out tea with extra lemon cake," She winked at Hyacinth and Gregory. "And of course there's lemonade if you're feeling parched from the journey."

"Are Ben and Calvin here yet?" Hyacinth piped up.

"They're not arriving till tomorrow, I'm afraid. Their break starts later."

"No matter," Anthony supplied. "Abigail managed to talk me into a dog, he should be around here some-where." He turned back to the house and yelled, "Nicki! Where are you?"

Out of the grand entrance came bounding a golden re-triever puppy. Hyacinth and Gregory practically jumped on him with all the adoration in their eyes.

Sighing, Abby turned back to everyone else, "Shall we?" And she gestured back towards the grounds where tea was all set.

As they walked, Daphne handed August off to Simon and jogged forward to link arms with Abigail.

"So, any news to share with me?" Daphne was astounding how she could just pick and choose when she wanted to be subtle and when she didn't.

"Meaning?" Abigail played coy.

Elbowing her in the ribs Daphne gave her a pointed look before continuing.

"You know exactly what I mean." She dropped her voice to an excited whisper. "Are you yet with child?"

"Well, if I was, I believe I should tell my husband first before I tell you, hm?"

Daphne gasped and stepped back with her hands over her mouth. She let out an excited squeal. Exactly the opposite of subtle, and Abby shushed her.

"What's going on up there?" Anthony called, from where he was walking with his mother.

"Nothing!" Daphne responded too quickly. "Just um, excited for Abby's first Pall-Mall game."

Abigail gave her a look before diverting her attentions.

"I don't know. If this is anything like I've been warned, I should be more nervous than excited."

They had all made it to the table and were pouring themselves either tea or lemonade. Simon handed the baby to his mother-in-law, who was gesturing for him.

"I'm with Abigail." Simon chimed in. "I'm growing rather intimidated based off of the vague threats I've heard you all exchange."

"Were we being vague?" Eloise turned towards her brothers.

"No, I don't believe so." Benedict responded. "I've already heard Anthony threatened to do something with the wickets that I shall not repeat."

"Might I put in a word we at least start civil, so as not to scare the new in-laws." Colin finally said.

"Thank you, Colin." Said Abby.

"Fine." Anthony obliged. "Daph, why don't you give some pointers while I go set the course."

"Who says you get to set the course?" Eloise questioned.

"I'm with her. You're vindictive when you get to be in charge." Benedict added.

"How about," Abby said, sensing an argument brewing before they even started. "Daphne explains the rules while you each take two wickets and set the course yourselves."

"Thank god you married her." Colin didn't bother to keep his voice down as he grabbed two wickets from Anthony.

"Heard that." Anthony followed him.

"Well, I said it loud."

Daphne simply rolled her eyes and faced her husband and best friend.

"Now, Pall-Mall is less about rules, and more about the goal. Which is, of course to hit your ball through each wicket." Simon nodded in understanding, and Abigail was tempted to salute her for how seriously she was taking this.

"The first player to send their ball though the last wicket wins. Simple enough." She looked pointedly at Abigail now. "Though, if you are feeling devilish, which I would recommend as your husband is the worst of us all, you can use your turn to knock an opponents ball as far away as you would like."

"Duly noted." Abigail smirked.

"Right, now," Daphne turned to face her siblings heading back from placing their wickets. "Benedict is a solid shot but he avoids conflict. Colin is crafty; he will strike when he thinks you are least suspecting it, so always be suspecting it. Eloise concentrates entirely on defeating her older brothers."

She faced them once again.

"I, of course, am a complete enigma who will divulge none of my secrets."

Simon chuckled and gazed at his wife.

"I'm sure." He said, with enough sarcasm in his voice to make Daphne raise a brow at him.

Turning back towards Abby she finished her instructions with, "I'm sure you have your husband figured out enough to know that he is the most cut-through player.

"Oh I've gathered that. He's been talking about this game for weeks."

"Have I?" Anthony joined them as they all arrived back at the tea tent.

"Yes, you have." She chuckled at him.

It had grown annoying at times, but in its own, odd way it was really endearing.

"Alright, now can we get started?" Eloise was practically bouncing on her toes.

"I don't see why not." Anthony was similar to his sister in that he was also itching to get going.

"Ah!" Daphne stopped them all before they made it to the mallet stand. "I believe, in the effort of starting civil, the new comers should get to pick their mallets first."

"Ah is that what we are now? New comers?" Simon stood next to Abby as he teased.

"It's as if we just got here." Abigail added, playing along.

"If you don't want the advantage..." Anthony started.

"Not so fast!" Both Simon and Abby said in unison.

They both approached the mallet stand and at least Abigail enjoyed hearing the groaning from Eloise about how long they were taking.

Finally, Simon picked first, grabbing the red mallet. He had clearly picked his favorite color, and Abigail couldn't blame him. She too, had a lucky color. But at the moment she was looking to see which mallet would annoy her husband the most. She landed on the black one.

Immediately, she knew she had chosen correctly as every sibling let out a hushed murmur.

"The mallet of death." Said Colin. "Would you look at that, brother?"

"Oh." Abigail feigned ignorance. "Is this yours?"

"You cheeky..." He shook his head at her.

She had evidently been paying more attention than he thought.

Taking a deep breath he said, "No. Not at all, you're welcome to it, love."

Benedict scoffed.

"You threatened to beat me the last time I touched—"

"You exaggerate." Anthony cut him off.

"My husband, superstitious. Will you be alright? I know some men cannot perform without their usual tools... like a child with a blanket." She saw no point in wasting time, so she cut right to the competitive jabs.

"Are we going to stand here deliberating all day, or shall we play?" Eloise groaned.

No sooner had the words left her lips than the siblings rounded on the mallet stand. Everyone managed

their preferred mallet, except Anthony. He had evidently been too distracted by his wife.

He held a look of annoyance as all he held up the last
and only mallet left. The pink one.

"To the field of combat!" Daphne shouted and they all
marched forward.

——-

They had all been playing for about an hour, everyone
performing on a different level. Daphne's narration of
each Bridgerton's style had proven to be correct. Colin
had knocked Abby's ball far away when she least expected it.

She knew there was no chance of winning now. In fact,
she had never intended to try and win. Every sibling took
this very seriously and she thoroughly enjoyed throwing
them off course.

She and Simon had formed a sort of in-law alliance and
were simply using their turns to cause pure chaos now.

This time, Abby thought she might have gone too far.
She hadn't immediately targeted Anthony as that would
have been too expected. First she had hit Eloise, then
Colin (revenge tasted sweet), and she had just now gotten to her husband. Trouble is, she knocked it a little too
hard and it had flown into the tree line just in front of
them.

Anthony was vindictive and his turn was immediately after hers. He too, knocked her ball into the tree line.

"What a shame." Colin piped up. "Guess you two had better go and fetch them. Unless you'd like to quit here and now?"

"Absolutely not." Anthony answered for the both of them and dragged her off with him towards the tree line. They were fully covered within the woods when Abby finally spoke.

"Alright, alright! I'm following you." She was laughing at his persistence.

But in less than a second the wind was knocked out of her as Anthony grabbed her whole body and pushed her against the nearest tree, his hands keeping her from moving.

"I ought to punish you for how you've been acting."

The change in atmosphere was so sudden Abigail couldn't get her thoughts straight.

"I... um—"

"Choosing my mallet, targeting me throughout the game... your own husband." He feigned astonishment.

His hands were working magic, knowing exactly where to roam. His lips were worse, though. Performing a dance around hers that only seemed to make her ache for him even more.

"I ought to be furious..."

So close. So damn close.

Then, as swiftly as he had made contact, he removed it. He was off of her and swinging his pink mallet onto his shoulder, chuckling to himself at her stunned expression.

"Come on, they must be further in the wood."

She regained her breath with some difficulty and narrowed her eyes after him.

Catching up she only muttered, "That was cruel." Before spotting what they came for.

"Ladies first." Anthony said, still awfully proud of himself.

As she hit her ball back into the field, she could only think of one thing that would throw him off his game now: the truth that ought to come out of its silence.

So, as Anthony raised his mallet and began to swing downwards, his focus rivaling that of a trained soldier, she said,

"I'm pregnant."